B L I N K

A New Line Cinema Production
A Michael Apted Film
MADELEINE STOWE • AIDAN QUINN
BLINK
JAMES REMAR • PETER FRIEDMAN
BRUCE A. YOUNG And LAURIE METCALF

Production Designer **Dan Bishop** Music by **Brad Fiedel**

Editor **Rick Shaine** Director of Photography **Dante Spinotti A.I.C.**

Executive Producers **Robert Shaye, Sara Risher**

Written by **Dana Stevens** Produced by **David Blocker**

Directed by **Michael Apted**

BLINK

**A novel by Tom Philbin
Based upon the screenplay
by Dana Stevens**

JOVE BOOKS, NEW YORK

BLINK

A Jove Book / published by arrangement with
New Line Productions, Inc.

PRINTING HISTORY
Jove edition / January 1994

ISBN: 0-515-11397-2

A JOVE BOOK®
Jove Books are published by The Berkley Publishing Group,
200 Madison Avenue, New York, New York 10016.
JOVE and the "J" design are trademarks
belonging to Jove Publications, Inc.

PRINTED IN THE UNITED STATES OF AMERICA

10 9 8 7 6 5 4 3 2 1

BLINK

1

· · ·

ON THE POORLY LIT STREET WHERE O'FLAHERTY'S
Pub was located all the stores were closed, and
there were no pedestrians and no vehicular traffic.

It was lonely.

And cold, a typical February night in Chicago,
which was not known for balmy weather. At midnight the temperature was ten degrees and heading
south.

Inside O'Flaherty's was another story. The relatively small room was hot, smoky, brimming with
life and sound, packed with more than four hundred
people (indeed the fire marshal would have cleared
it because the room's capacity was three hundred if
the pub's owner didn't pay him not to), a number
of them step dancing—an Irish dance where the
dancers resemble puppets being manipulated by a
demented puppeteer—to an Irish jig being pumped
out by a band on a platform above the dance floor.

At the center of all this life was a fiddler, not a ruddy-faced Irishman but a beautiful woman with delicate features, full lips, perfect teeth, long brown hair, and a tight-fitting dress that encased and accented a beautiful body. Her left hand fingered the strings on her violin with stunning dexterity and speed, her bow rising and falling rapidly and producing a foot-tapping sound that one patron had commented was so suffused with life that "it would make the deceased get up and start to dance."

Random comments, delivered by various drunks in the crowd, could be heard.

"Mother Mary," said one, "look at her."

"Look at the glands," said another, "on that motherfucker."

Small tables ringed the dance floor and at one of them, relatively close to the platform, sat five men, four youngish and one middle-aged, their small table crowded with empty Old Style beer bottles. A blond-haired waitress was in the process of partially clearing them so she could deliver four more of the same.

The beautiful fiddler had not escaped the attention of the men either. One of them in particular, a handsome man with light blue eyes and curly brown hair who bore more than a passing resemblance to a young Paul Newman, seemed mesmerized by the woman. He stared at her, unblinking. The oldest of the men, whose name was Mitchell, and who was a dark-haired dude with a face that looked like it had been hit with an entrenching tool and that wore a perpetual expression of displeasure, spoke to the handsome man, whose name was John.

"Is she one of your people?"

John hardly heard Mitchell. His eyes were going up and down the fiddler's body and face, not quite trusting the evidence of his eyes. She was the most glorious example of female pulchritude he had ever seen.

Mitchell tried again. "You a mick, John? You drink like a mick."

"You kidding," Ned said. "That face? He's fuckin' Mickey O'Malley."

"My mother's side," John finally said. "Cleary. County Cork."

"Your mother look like that?" asked Crowe, a handsome young man with blond hair, nodding toward the beautiful fiddler.

John did not answer. He was back to his major preoccupation.

"I gotta know that girl," he said.

With that, he drew out his wallet and plucked a ten from it. Then he got up and weaved and staggered his way through the crowd to the stage, singing and laughing all the while, and dropped the ten in a giant snifter at the foot of the stage.

He stood a moment, but the fiddler didn't acknowledge him, though one of the band members waved.

"Real subtle," said Barry to John when he got back to the table.

"You guys have to be subtle," John said. "You're married."

"She doesn't like you," Barry said.

"No wonder," said Ned, "that suit."

John turned to Ned and put his thumb under the lapel of the light brown suit. "What's wrong with my suit?"

"You oughta have a matching handbag," Ned said.

3

"How much did that thing cost? Two paychecks?"

"Ned, you buy your suits at Mervyns. You get your girls there too."

"The girls work hard at Mervyn's, show some respect."

"Oh," Barry said, "my knight in shining armor, is that how you get chicks to fuck you?"

"Chicks fuck me 'cause they like me, Barry, because I like 'em," said John.

" 'Cause your gonads," Mitchell said, "are bigger than your brain."

" 'Cause I don't got girlie mags," John said, referring to Barry, "on the coffee table. You been to this guy's apartment. When was the last time you got laid, Barry—Carter-Mondale?"

"I'll bet you twenty bucks you can't nab that girl on stage," Ned said to John.

"Twenty bucks. I'm not gonna find that handbag for less than fifty."

Abruptly, John stood up and got off a piercing wolf whistle. "You're beautiful. You with the fiddle! I'm in love."

Band members looked, but not the fiddler. John was yanked down by the tail of his suit jacket.

"I'll bet you fifty," Mitchell said, his face showing a glint of pleasure. "I'll bet you fifty you can't even get her to smile in your direction."

John stared at them all—all laughing.

"I'm in for that one," Ned said.

John nodded and got up. He took his suit jacket off, then his shirt, and then moved away from the table and onto the dance floor, the striptease continuing as he was surrounded by appreciative dancers while he took off his T-shirt and his belt.

The cheers got louder with each item, and Ned made the perfect observation:

"Mad fuckin' bastard."

But John didn't stop. He dropped his pants and gyrated around, the crowd urging him to take his shorts off, while quite a few of the women in the audience ooohed and ahhed about the hard, muscular body they were being treated to. Finally, the fiddler turned her head toward the noise and commotion, and John looked into her eyes and, as drunk as he was, was shocked by the glazed, milky whiteness of them.

The beautiful fiddler was blind.

AN HOUR AFTER the strip show, three members of the band—Michael, Sean, and Winston—were loading their instruments into a van parked near the pub.

The fiddler, whose name was Emma Brody, stood waiting, her violin case in hand, a yellow Labrador guide dog standing next to her.

"Emma finally got a groupie," Sean said.

"Ralph's my groupie," Emma said, patting the dog.

Then Candice Archer, manager of the band, came out of the club door and walked towards Michael.

Candice was pretty, in her early thirties, buried in a cacophony of stylistic flourishes including spiked hair and earrings down to her shoulders, her scent heavy with patchouli oil.

She was beaming as she came up to Emma.

"Great show, baby," she said, "That *Sun-Times* reporter was here, and she may have been dancing. Either she was dancing or she stepped in some gum."

"Hey, Candice," Emma said, greeting her.

"Who was that asshole?" Candice said.

"What did he do?" Emma asked.

"He gave us a great big anatomy lesson," Candice said.

"How big?" Emma asked, and the group laughed.

2
. . .

Forty-five minutes after she left O'Flaherty's, Emma negotiated the two blocks from the Fullerton station of the elevated train—or El as it was called in Chicago—to her home on the near North Side. It was a small apartment in one of a number of small brick apartment houses on Milwaukee Street. It was two A.M., par for the course for any working musician, including those who worked for peanuts but mainly subsisted on dreams of success.

As she walked, a variety of clichés occurred to her to describe the weather. "Cold as a witch's tit," she thought, would do nicely. She even imagined that Ralph, who walked at her side as she held the harness, wanted to get in out of the cold. *That* was cold.

Emma had no trouble reading the environment with the senses she had available to her—hearing, touch, smell, and taste—and no trouble finding her way home safely (with, of course, Ralph's assistance).

She could stand on a street corner and hear a light change, knowing from the quality and quantity of sounds issuing from its mechanical stomach if it was red or green, whether she could walk or not; she could hear cars coming, going, stopping, and from their smell, could know whether they needed a tune-up. And her nose could forecast the weather.

Tonight there was a tomorrow-snow smell in the air. It would come down, she thought, very lightly . . . perhaps an inch or two.

Too bad, she had often thought, she couldn't get a part-time job as a weatherperson. Certainly she would do better than the guys on WGN, who were pulling in about a half of mil a year to tell what tomorrow's weather would be, and were wrong one third of the time. Yeah, they might go for it. "And now here's Emma Brody, who can really be said to have a nose for weather news!"

Emma was alert, though the neighborhood was a relatively safe one. There had been a couple of burglaries over the three years she'd lived in her apartment, but no violent crime. If someone did approach her with malicious intent, she knew she would likely have only one shot, and she planned to triangulate exactly where the balls of the perpetrator were so she could kick them up into his pelvic cavity.

She climbed a few steps, and then was on the stoop of her building. She broke out a chain of keys, and her fingers found the one she needed as quickly as a sighted person might have.

8

She let herself in—the foyer was heated and felt wonderful—closed the door behind her, then used another key to let herself into the main hallway.

Here it was even hotter and the smells of the day hit her. After living in the building for three years, she knew which smells came from which of the twenty apartments in the five-story building: from old Mrs. Schmidt in 1A on the first floor, who was a German cook par excellence, to the incense and marijuana coming from the apartment of Valerie, a tall hippie girl who lived in 3B, directly above her.

But tonight there was a another smell in the hall. Someone was standing there without making a sound, and she would have been alarmed had it not been a familiar smell: one that came from the gnarled Italian cigars which, to Emma, should have been named shitsticks, which described their aroma quite accurately.

"Hello, Mr. Cuchetto," Emma said. He was the super, an old man who lived in 1B and had a few strange habits, among which was walking around the building at two in the morning.

"Emma," he said, a little wonder in his voice. He had told her once that he was amazed at how she could know so much without having eyes, and this had been a test of her ability . . . with the same surprising results.

SHE ENTERED HER second-floor apartment, 2B, with two keys, one for the regular lock, one for the jimmy-proof dead bolt.

Inside, she kicked off her shoes, unharnessed Ralph, and went down a short hall. If this wasn't the night for a cup of herbal tea, she didn't know what was. She went into the kitchen and turned on the front gas jet, the little pop and hiss telling her the burner was on. She rinsed out a small teapot, then half filled it and set it on the burner.

She went out of the kitchen directly through an archway into the living room and turned on the TV, which of course she couldn't see but could hear. It was like having someone live with you. You were never alone, though there were times when she sensed she could pick a better companion.

She sat down on a giant clawfoot couch, its ugliness flickeringly illuminated by the TV. It was upholstered in soft silk-satin, the print a blend of orange and green.

Unhappily, it melded well with the rest of the decor, a melange featuring a kitchen table made of knotty pine, kitchen chairs covered in woven blankets of wooden beads, a tattered red velveteen armchair, and a thin coffee table in front of the couch. Nothing matched in color, texture, or size. One of her friends had described it as "Early Eclectic, the work of a diseased mind." Emma's explanation was simply that she didn't give a shit what it looked like, because it all looked the same to her.

On TV, a WGN sports guy was doing a taped recap of the night in Chicago sports, lamenting the retirement of Michael Jordan in a close game between the Bulls and the Pistons.

Ralph came lumbering into the room, in his mouth a beat-up stuffed bunny and a bag of cookies. Emma took the cookies, fished one out, and started to munch.

The phone rang, but the lateness of the call did not rattle her. There was no limit to a musician's hours.

The phone was on an adjacent coffee table, and her hand homed in on the receiver without a scintilla of hesitation.

"Hello."

"It's Dr. Pierce."

Dr. Pierce was someone she had met some two months earlier, someone who had become interested in her eyesight.

"Doc, it's Saturday night. Why aren't you on a date?"

"I don't have dates. I have seminars. Emma . . . we have a pair of eyes."

Something in Emma moved, a surge of excitement, and fear.

"From a donor brought in tonight," Pierce continued. "I pulled a few strings at the eye bank."

"What are you saying?"

"Would you like to do it now?"

Emma could not talk—but the kettle did, starting to emit a high-pitched shriek, helping to emphasize the jangling chaos inside her.

3
• • •

THIRTY MINUTES LATER, AFTER A FAST RIDE
through almost empty streets in a cab, Emma
stood by the admitting counter of Booth Memorial Hospital and tried to give personal information to a receiving nurse. Tried to, because
the stuff that had started to surge inside her
had not let up. Her stomach felt like Jell-O.

"247 Milwaukee, 2B?" the heavyset black nurse
said.

Emma pondered, but didn't answer. Just at that
moment a bookish but handsome man pulled up with
a wheelchair. It was Doctor Ryan Pierce. He helped
Emma into the chair, his every movement indicating
the depth of his concern.

"247 Milwaukee, what?" the nurse repeated.

Pierce turned around the form the nurse was writing on and rapidly scribbled on it.

"She's been waiting twenty years," he said not

unkindly to the nurse, "and you want her to fill out forms."

"I think you're as excited about this as I am," Emma said.

Pierce, a man who was hardly the type for one-liners, got one off. "I'm getting new wallpaper in the office and I just have to have your opinion."

Emma laughed heartily.

AN HOUR LATER, Emma was on a gurney being wheeled down a corridor toward the operating room.

Now she was at peace, in no small part due to the Valium being pumped into her from a mobile IV unit that rolled along next to the gurney. Dr. Pierce was beside her, his hand touching her.

Phrases she had just heard as she was being prepped for the surgery came to mind . . . "lens implant and corneal graft . . . microscope to OR eight . . ."

From afar, she heard only the voice of Dr. Pierce, but she knew he was not alone.

"Just relax, Emma. Count sheep."

Emma took a moment before speaking. Her thoughts were not all that clear, and her mouth felt a little like lead.

"I don't remember sheep," she said. "I keep picturing Wile E. Coyote."

"Count. Something you know a lot of."

Emma laughed sexily.

"Not men, thank you," he said. "How 'bout your jobs?"

"Uh . . . okay. Uh, carton packer, ticket taker,

13

seamstress, dispatcher, suicide hotline, trainer of tiny dogs, typist, gift wrapper, uh, hooker . . . not really."

The gurney made a turn, and she heard doors swinging open and then a new smell: the sharp smell of alcohol . . . the operating room.

Emma felt herself slipping off an edge, from something black to something even blacker, and she thought she should be more afraid than she was, and not just about the operation. But she was not.

Then, her eyes fluttered and closed, and she fell off the edge of the world.

4
...

JOHN, THE STRIPTEASE ARTIST AT O'FLAHERTY'S, peeked out from under the warm covers, but shifted his head before opening his eyes. The sun was in them.

As he did, he looked around the room and wondered: Where the fuck am I?

The room was a wonderland of chintz and femininity, the curtains lined with lace, a vanity and dresser pale pink, the rug white and delicate-looking, the walls mauve—except for one wall covered with white paper featuring a delicate rose pattern.

He became aware of the smell, a blend of methane and alcohol, and then of his head, which had started to rhythmically pound.

He swallowed—or tried to. His mouth felt glued shut, as if the last drink he had had before going to bed—and he was aware that he had imbibed heavily—had been a shot of thinned Elmer's Carpenter's Glue.

He started to turn over and his hand touched warm flesh. Carefully, sensing where he was, because he had been in this situation many times before, he turned and looked into the face of the waitress who had served them at O'Flaherty's the night before.

Faces of Death, Part V.

No, not that bad, he thought, but definitely a few beauty clicks removed from what he must have perceived the night before. The flattish features were riddled with rivulets of wrinkles around the eyes and mouth and across the forehead, the tanning-salon tan seeming to accent them. The face was puffy, particularly the lips, which were smeared with lipstick. Mascara had run down from one eye like a blue tear, and there were black roots at the base of the stark-blond hair.

He had a vague memory of fucking, sucking, how good she tasted.

How good she tasted? Jesus.

He had to get out of here without waking her, even though he was about to be curdled a bit inside. He had an image of himself in O'Flaherty's butt-ass naked, waving to a beautiful fiddler.

He remembered her. The fiddler. The frustration. The need to unload into somebody.

When the waitress's thighs—he couldn't think of her name—had been flanking his face, he'd thought she was the fiddler.

He looked again. She was not the fiddler. He had to get the fuck out of here. He slithered out from under the Laura Ashley comforter and realized he was still wearing a condom. Used.

Nice.

JOHN STEPPED OUT of the door onto a small porch, fronted by a small yard surrounded by a short cyclone fence.

The cold and glare hit him immediately. It had snowed lightly—in fact, there were still a few random flakes falling—and the bright white yard and street served as a mirror for the morning sun, making him shade his eyes.

He managed to spot a street sign some twenty yards away. Chartrain Street. He was familiar with the city and knew exactly where he was.

He started to walk away, and was almost out the gate, then turned back, stopped—his head pounding with particular savagery—and picked up a folded, plastic-encased newspaper that had been tossed onto the path.

A kid about ten standing in an adjacent yard asked the usual kind of direct question—sans formality or sensitivity—that kids asked.

"Are you the new Mr. Whitney?"

"No, kid," John responded. "I'm Santa, don't you recognize me?"

"Santa already came. At Christmas."

"Yeah, well, I had one more gift for Mrs. Whitney."

John passed through the gate, and turned towards Chartrain, going past the kid.

"You got one for me?"

"No."

"Why not?"

" 'Cause you're a bad kid."

"But Mrs. Whitney was good?"

"I have no idea, kid. No idea."

17

That really was the bottom line. He hoped he had had a wonderful time.

Then, abruptly, he thought again of the fiddler.

He closed his own eyes as he remembered her looking his way. That milky whiteness. Blind.

Christ.

Ahead was a coffee shop. He had to get some coffee into him, dilute the Elmer's.

He wondered where the fiddler was, what she was doing. He would bet she was still beautiful even when he was sober.

Then he turned his attention to the paper.

5
. . .

Emma felt as if she were in a movie, in a scene that she had seen many times over the years. In it the blind heroine was going to find out if she was ever going to see again.

But this was real, as indicated by the fact that she could feel her heart going like a triphammer, and her hands felt squishy.

She was in a hospital room, sitting on a straight-back chair, and Dr. Pierce was sitting on a wheeled chair in front of her. The room was cool and dim, sunlight framing opaque shades that covered the window.

They were not alone. Emma knew there were others in the room, a couple of doctors and nurses, people who would be caring for her, all of whom were interested in her case.

They had come to see the movie.

19

Dr. Pierce was about to unwrap the gauze and patch from the eye he had operated on. Unlike many doctors, he had given her a detailed blow-by-blow description of what was happening to her.

He had sewn a corneal graft on her left eye, the cornea—the dime-sized piece of clear tissue on the outside of the eyeball—having been damaged when she was young.

In fact, both eyes were damaged, but he had told her that when it came to grafts, it was best to see if there was any problem with rejection before doing the other eye. Most grafts, in fact, were up to ninety-percent successful, depending on the underlying cause, because the human cornea contained no blood vessels and there was no need to match donor with patient for blood compatability, or even use immunosupression therapy.

Multiple layers of gauze were wrapped around Emma's head. She imagined she looked like someone who had just come out of a battle and had sustained a head wound.

Emma's mind was a pinball machine, animated with a wide variety of thoughts going this way and that, but the one that unnerved and surprised her was that she hoped the operation had not been a success. She liked being blind. Being blind was a world she had learned to handle. Living in a sighted world was a whole other thing.

Of course she also wanted to see very, very badly. She would take her chances.

"Some of the staff are here to observe," Dr. Pierce said.

"Bobby, are you there?"

A handsome young man dressed in whites made a slight movement forward.

"I'm here, Emma."

" 'Cause I want to know what you look like."

"You won't be sorry."

The observers laughed, but beneath the laughter was the nervousness. Emma Brody had not seen anything in twenty years.

Slowly and deliberately, working with his hands and surgical scissors, Dr. Pierce started to remove the bandages.

"What's the first thing I'll see?" she asked.

"Probably my face," Pierce said.

"Leave the bandage on."

Then something surged in Emma. Something dark.

"Stop!" Emma suddenly blurted out, pushing Pierce's hands away.

She was breathing rapidly.

"I'm scared."

"It's scary," Pierce said.

Emma paused. "Could you ask those others to leave?"

She heard a shuffling towards the door, and then the room was empty except for her and Dr. Pierce.

"That was a joke. About your face."

"I know."

"I just wish I'd seen it before. So I could prepare myself."

"Picture the last one you saw."

A steel fist squeezed Emma's innards. "It was my mother's. I hope I never have to see a face like that."

Pierce touched her face, waited. Emma placed her hands in her lap. A moment later he began to unwind the last of the gauze, and removed the eye patch, thick with salve . . .

"Don't expect too much at first. It's just the one eye."

Very gently he swabbed her eyes with a cotton ball.

"I'm going to open the lids."

Using a finger, he raised the lid of the eye he had operated on . . .

It was weird—but wonderful. Hanging in front of Emma was a huge painting, totally flat. There was Pierce, the walls, the entry to the bathroom, the wall on one flat plain.

But *there*.

Tears misted her eyes, her heart rate elevated.

Her perspective shifted, and some of the objects appeared larger than others.

At the center of the picture appeared large square white blocks. Teeth. Pierce's teeth. He was smiling.

She reached for his mouth, her hand coming into the picture in front of her.

She missed—completely. His mouth was nine miles away.

"You have no depth perception now," Pierce said.

She hardly heard him. She was too fascinated by the spectacle, the wonder of moving lips.

"Here I am," he said. He took her hand. His hand was warm. He guided it to his face. A soft, warm face.

"Hello, Dr. Pierce," Emma said. "Nice, uh, nice to . . . see you."

She released a puff of laughter, and then a flood of tears. They fell into an embrace. The movie seemed to have had a happy ending.

6

. . .

THE NIGHT OF THE DAY DR. PIERCE REMOVED THE
bandages, Emma lay in the bed in her dimly lit
hospital room. She was about to embark on a major
exploration: find the bathroom.

No way, she thought, could the vision she had
be considered normal. Twenty years ago she was
sighted, and it was not like this. This was weird,
as if the entire room, her entire world was reflected,
refracted in funhouse mirrors—pieces and parts of
pieces, bloated and misshapen, the light fixture
seeming to be a spaceship that had melted in
the heat and drooped, the bars above the bed like
sections of a dotted lines . . . in sum, Daliesque.

She felt edgy. This was really the first time she
would attempt to navigate on her own.

She sat up, the disjointed world swinging up with
her, and sat on the edge of the bed. She waited for the
world to settle, to come together, but it did not.

Shakily, she stood up—and it got worse. The parts and pieces of the world started to move, to expand and contract. Instinctively, she reached out, trying to calm the world—and it didn't help.

She took one step, another, in the direction of the bathroom, anxiety escalating as she did.

She felt a spurt of panic. She was not going to make it.

She closed her eyes, and the disjointed world went away. She was back to blackness—and calm, relaxation oozing through her body like Valium.

She walked the few steps to the bathroom, went inside the little room.

She found the light switch and flicked it on.

She opened her eyes—and gasped. Her image leaped out at her from the cabinet mirror, but it was inanimate pieces of her face sort of strewn around, the only living part her dark brown irises, hanging alone, watching her.

The light seared her eyes. She wanted to keep looking, to fight through it, but she couldn't. She turned and backed out of the bathroom, then turned and looked towards the door to the room, which had been closed. Someone had opened it.

Emma opened her eyes. Light from the hall reflected in Emma's eyes.

"Is someone there?"

Candice Archer was standing there, a bouquet of flowers in her hands.

She did not answer.

"Hello?" Emma said.

Again, no answer. Her eyes flicked this way and that. Nothing.

Then Candy was gone. The door clicked shut.

● ● ●

A few minutes later, far down the hall, Candice Archer was following Dr. Pierce down the hall, gesticulating with the bouquet as she did.

She was not happy.

"I walked into her room just now and she looked right through me. She couldn't even tell if there was anyone there! What the fuck kind of a . . . can I say fuck here?"

"I . . ." Dr. Pierce began, but Candice knifed in.

"What the fuck kind of a doctor are you?"

"I'm an ocular surgeon, and I can't discuss Emma's case with anyone but Emma. Or family."

"The band is her family. We have this interview."

"She can't handle that yet," Dr. Pierce said as he pushed his way through the front door out of the building.

"She's been on her own since she was fifteen," Candice countered. "She handles a lot."

"She wants you to think that."

Candice nodded knowingly.

"You want to take care of her," she said. "Men react that way to Emma."

"I do take care of her. I'm her doctor."

"Can she see or not, *Doctor*?" Candice said, her mouth curled a little.

Pierce stopped at his car, a vintage sporty, apple-red Mercedes.

"You know," he said, "what it's like to be sleeping when someone turns on the lights. How it hurts. How you squint and stumble around and it takes you some time to adjust? Effectively, Emma's been sleeping for twenty years. Humans reach visual maturity at age

25

nine. Emma was blinded at eight. We just don't know what she'll see, or how well she'll see it."

"Is this your car?" Candice said, her voice edged with sarcasm as if to say . . . do you deserve it?

7

. . .

In her dreams, Emma had always been able to
see, but the scenes were from her childhood. She
had no picture of herself when she was older: That
person didn't exist when she became blind.

The curious thing about the dreams was that most
of them were pleasant, which hardly reflected what
her childhood was like. Perhaps it was because none
of the people of her childhood days, chiefly her mother, was present.

But this dream was unpleasant, and she wasn't
exactly sure what was happening. It came in bits and
pieces, with Emma feeling threatened, but the most
curious thing of all was that it was conducted in the
dark. She somehow realized that she was not totally
blind anymore, but this did not make sense.

Then, abruptly, the dream ended—and she became
aware that she was in her hospital room. She was
under the covers and . . .

The door opened, and standing in it was a good-looking woman rather unusually dressed, the smell of patchouli oil strong. She was holding a beautiful bouquet of flowers and was smiling broadly.

Emma did not recognize Candice.

"Hello. Can I help you," Emma said.

There was no response, just the smiling face. And then the smile faded and Emma looked down and stripped the sheets off to get out of bed, and when she looked up the door was closed. The person had left.

Emma felt a spurt of anxiety, confusion.

What the fuck was going on? She started to get out of bed. The door opened and she started to try to walk, and misjudged something and started to fall—and Dr. Pierce caught her.

"Em . . . hey. Good morning."

"There was a woman in here, just now, a pretty woman with flowers . . ."

"Candice?"

"You saw her? Was that . . . ? That's Candice, huh? Tell her to come back."

"It was yesterday, Emma."

"Yesterday?" Emma said.

"Candice was here yesterday."

"Yesterday, then . . ." Her voice trailed off.

Emma touched her face. She glanced towards the bathroom. A vague, fleeting memory . . . a fear . . .

What—*what*—what the fuck was going on.

Pierce nodded. He paused, then spoke. "There is some research out there about a perceptual delay. In the early days of the surgery."

"I don't get it."

"Like a flashback. You see something new, but you don't understand what it is until the next day."

28

"You think that's what happened?"

"No. I think you were dreaming."

"What's the difference?"

Pierce said nothing. Emma looked at him. She almost smiled. She longed for the days when she was totally blind.

8
. . .

Emma felt vaguely like an astronaut. She was sitting—or lying back—on a space-age–style hydraulic chair which Dr. Pierce was operating, gradually tilting her backward.

Then she was in position and, wearing an ophthalmoscope, a circular black headpiece with an intense light, Dr. Pierce looked carefully at the retinas of her eyes.

Satisfied, he leaned back.

"The eye bank has another cornea."

"It's only been five weeks."

"We got lucky."

One day after he examined her, Dr. Pierce "did" Emma's other eye, and a couple of days later he examined her again. As he did, he spoke.

"Your second eye is healing well. But the next few months might be tough. You may experience a wavering, in and out of focus. You may be able to see sharply in your peripheral vision, while the central vision remains blurry. Or things may suddenly jump into focus. Other than that, you're ready to go."

"Go where?"

"Home. I'll see you tomorrow."

He had been sitting on a wheeled stool as he examined her. He pushed away.

"This is it?" Emma said. "I want my money back."

Before she left Dr. Pierce prescribed an ointment for her eyes, and cautioned her to avoid rubbing them or any bending or other activities that would put pressure on her eyes.

Then she left on her own, to go out, as it were, to see the world . . . a happy, but at the same time very scary, prospect.

9
● ● ●

EMMA DID NOT GO DIRECTLY HOME, BUT INSTEAD, at the request of Candice, she went to a house on Charlton Street which the band used as a command post—home, recording studio, and office. Candice, of course, had an ulterior motive—she wanted Emma to sit for an interview.

A reception committee was waiting outside the slightly run-down red brick building when Emma arrived. Emma could see fairly well. All the members of the band were there, and Candice, and a woman Emma assumed was the reporter.

There was also someone else there who made her fill up with happiness like a balloon.

Ralph.

Instantly, Emma was down on her haunches and Ralph was slobbering over her—and she over Ralph.

"Hi, baby! Hi, baby boy!"

As she did, she just barely heard Candice say: "Emma, this is my friend from the *Chicago Sun-Times.*"

The woman, who had a pencil threaded in her hair, was dressed all in black—and in attitude. Emma was not impressed, but she did know that the interview was important. Just the kind of thing, Candice had suggested, that would be noticed by the right people and could catapult the band to bigger and better things.

THE COMMAND POST could hardly be described as a state-of-the-art media center. The living room was littered with all kinds of paper, the walls were festooned with all kinds of notes and flyers and God-knows-what-all, and the sounds emanating from the house were equally chaotic. From somewhere came the sound of an electric guitar, and a rumbling old Xerox machine in the living room was in the process of spitting out flyers.

The interview started as the group entered the apartment, Emma explaining that Dr. Ryan Pierce had seen her perform and his trained eye had detected that she responded to certain light shifts, indicating that she was not totally blind and that he might be able to do something for her, just because he was a caring kind of doctor.

When he'd examined her he'd discovered there was hope—more than hope.

"It wasn't," Emma said, "just corneal transplants. He also implanted synthetic lenses."

The reporter nodded, keeping her own eyes engaged in the business of picking her way through fast-food wrappers and other debris on the floor as they passed through the living room.

They proceeded into the kitchen, which had some semblance of cleanliness and order.

"What was your condition, the technical terms?"

For a moment Emma was distracted, a little jealous. The reporter was perched on a countertop and Emma could not help but notice the sleek, sexy legs and high heels, comparing them to her own legs, somehow seeming dumpy in the pleated skirt she wore.

"What was your condition, the technical terms?"

"I had traumatic cataracts and severely damaged corneas."

"From . . ."

"My mother smashed my head into a mirror."

"Why?"

"I wasn't supposed to play with her makeup."

For a moment, Emma was mesmerized by the color of the makeup on the reporter's face, and she touched her own face.

"These surgeries have been fairly routine for years now," the reporter said. "How come you didn't know about them before?"

"I thought my retinas were damaged. My mother, her doctors told me I would never see again."

"But now . . . you see . . . normally?"

"I don't know. Things are pretty jumbled, but every once in a while I see something crystal clear."

Emma paused. Something was surging inside her. "Are you," she said simply with feeling, "pretty? Do people say you're a pretty girl?"

"My boyfriend does."

Emma nodded. She wondered if she was pretty. It was not something she had thought about for a long time.

The questions went on for another fifteen minutes, and Emma recounted how after the event with her mother she had been adopted by foster parents, and that her stepfather had been a teacher of the violin. He'd started giving her instructions a few months after she arrived. Within two years she was a grade-six violinist—the highest level possible.

Then, when she was fifteen, first her stepfather, then her stepmother passed away, and she was on her own. She tried various occupations, and then she decided to make her living as a fiddler.

There were additional questions about her art, and she tried to explain to the reporter—and she seemed to understand—how not only was playing the violin about the mastery of a beautiful instrument, and the creation of beautiful music, but also about how it served as a place for her to go to when she was hurting. She could live inside the sound she produced, and nothing could touch her.

The interview seemed to have gone very well, and less than forty-five minutes after she had arrived she and Candice were saying good-bye on the street, and Candice confirmed that she thought the interview did go very well, and that the article would likely appear within the next two weeks.

Then they separated, Emma taking the El to her home, and as she did she felt very happy. Yet underlying this was a sense of something else.

Emma probed the why of it, but she wasn't really able to fix on an answer. All she knew was that it had something to do with regaining her sight . . . as if being able to see in life was going to make her see things in her head that she didn't want to see: Her eyes were like windows that looked outward—and inward.

More, what were these "flashbacks" that Dr. Pierce had spoken of? She had not told Pierce, but the experience with Candice had thoroughly frightened her. For one thing, it was as if she were psychotic, having no control over her thoughts. And secondly, what else would she experience? Pierce didn't seem to have any satisfactory answers. What if the flashbacks got bad? What if . . .

Emma cut herself off. If she continued to probe what might be she knew one thing for sure: She'd drive herself nuts.

She looked down at Ralph as she walked. She was so glad he was with her. He beat any tranquilizer she could buy.

10

• • •

E MMA WAS HOME, AND IT FELT GOOD.

She was standing at the bottom of the stairs inside her building, Ralph at her side.

Today, she thought, Mrs. Gold had made chicken soup, and Mr. Sanchez had cooked burritos. It was a potent combo, but at least it wasn't the smell of Mr. Cuchetto's cigars.

Emma could see well enough so that, she figured, she would try the stairs without Ralph's help. She had already exhorted Ralph to go up on his own. Ralph was confused. He had been as much a part of her as she of him.

"Go on, Ralph," she said gently.

Ralph looked up balefully at her.

"Go on up without me."

Then, proving again just how bright Labrador retrievers were, Ralph suddenly turned and clickety-clacked his way up the stairs, pausing at the first landing, tongue out, waiting for her.

Emma started up, gripping the handrail, relying on her eyes.

Halfway up, she miscalculated—and almost fell.

Vowing not to repeat that, she climbed another three steps . . . and almost fell again. It occurred to her that at this rate she would be heading back to the orthopedic section of Booth Memorial.

She closed her eyes, grasped the handrail, and was suddenly back in the familiar black world that she had lived in so long. She started to climb the steps flawlessly, Ralph leading the way on his own.

"Hey, I . . ." a voice said from the landing above her, startling Emma. Then she realized it was Valerie Wheaton, the nasty pot-smoking promiscuous hippie bitch who lived directly above her and played some of the shittiest music Emma had ever heard—loud and at all hours of the night.

Why, Emma thought, was she offering help? At any rate, she didn't want any.

"I don't need any help," Emma said sourly.

"I wasn't asking. The mailman put one of your letters in my box. I slipped it under your door."

Emma could see her clearly enough to make out the long dishwater-blond hair, and as she passed by her—getting a whiff of marijuana—she could see well enough to see that Valerie had stuck her tongue out. A brat.

Fuck you, Emma thought.

Then, Emma closed her eyes—and continued climbing the stairs flawlessly.

EMMA OPENED THE door to her apartment and Ralph bounded in, as glad to be home as she was. She went inside and closed the door behind her, locking both locks and slipping the chain in place. She stood in the foyer, looking into the living room.

Now, for the first time, she was able to see what being blind—and not caring—means when you're decorating an apartment. In sum, a cacophony of color, shape, and texture that added up to pain for the viewer.

"I think," she said out loud, "I understand the word tacky."

Ralph looked at her, and Emma imagined that he didn't have the heart to comment.

LATER THAT NIGHT, Emma was in her bedroom and stripped to her bra and panties. She was well aware that there was a full-length mirror on the back of the door. She was also aware that she had avoided looking into it.

She did. Nothing occurred, except she noted that it was not one of her moments of crystal-clear sight: She still looked like one of those Picasso paintings made up of flat, disjointed parts.

She also wanted to see what kind of outfits she had—she hoped they weren't in the same league as the decor—and started to take them out of the bedroom closet and try them on.

After a few minutes it became obvious how bad they were.

Discouraged, she walked to the bed and sat down, her image reflected in the mirror.

After a while she casually looked up—and gasped. In the mirror was not herself *now*, but as a little girl . . . herself at eight.

Her face had makeup on it like a clown, and she was

wearing her mother's clothing. She was putting more makeup on . . . and . . . Emma was terribly worried for her. She wanted to scream, "Watch out."

Then, behind the little girl a figure emerged from the shadows, and the face gradually came into focus . . . the twisted, enraged face of her mother. No, Mommy, no . . .

Emma slammed the door shut—and looked behind her. Nothing.

She was close to hyperventilating.

She stood up and did a quick sweep of the bed, gathering in all the outfits she had taken from the closet, and marched into the kitchen, where she stuffed them all in the trash can.

Then she went into the living room. There was one way, one place where, she knew, she could always retreat: inside the music of the violin . . .

She opened the case, extracted the bow and instrument . . . and suddenly realized that she couldn't see it that well. But she had to play. Had to . . .

She drew the bow across the strings . . . and the equivalent of a shriek emerged, a sound she might have made when she was first starting.

She tried again. There was no coordination between her bow and fingering hand.

She could not play.

She felt panic setting in. So she put the violin away and sat down in front of the TV, and turned it on with the remote control.

Or tried to. The picture was pure snow, the sound as annoying as a hundred pounds of bacon frying.

"Goddammit!" she yelled, and winged the remote device at the TV. It clunked off the glass and fell to the floor. The snow and frying bacon continued.

40

Shit, she thought, she wasn't going to spend the night like this. No fucking way.

She went into the kitchen and opened the refrigerator door.

A moment later she took out a half-gallon bottle of white wine. It was just what the doctor ordered.

11
· · ·

WHEN EMMA AWOKE SHE WAS NOT SURE SHE WAS really awake. Then she knew she was. Her head was pounding and she smelled like she had bathed in wine.

She also realized that she was lying on the couch in her house, an almost empty bottle of wine in one hand, the room illuminated only by the TV, which was still filled with snow, the sound now off. Otherwise it was dark.

She became aware that it was sometime in the middle of the night.

Then she became aware of something else. A sound. A thumping sound, from above. Directly above her. Valerie's apartment.

Suddenly she was fully awake.

Something crashed, a bang.

Jesus. She thought she heard a scream . . . part of one . . .

She got up and, woozy from the wine but alert, went across the room to the wall clock and felt the hands: 3:48.

She stood, looking up, as if she could see the source of the sound. Nothing. Maybe it was nothing. Maybe her mind was playing tricks again. Maybe.

She started to relax—then tensed. Another sound . . . a scraping sound . . .

CHHHHHH . . . CHHHHHH . . . CHHHHH . . .

No, not scraping, dragging. Something was being dragged across the floor.

Something. Or someone.

The sound stopped. Emma listened for more.

Nothing. Just the sound of water gurgling in a pipe, the distant bark of a dog.

It was quiet for a long time. She looked down. Ralph was there, by her side. Both were waiting for another sound.

Gooseflesh appeared. There was another sound. But not upstairs. Outside. In the hall.

She knew she should not open the door. No fucking way.

She walked over and as quietly as possible turned both locks, but left the chain on, and opened the door a crack and peered out.

It was dark, hard to see anything under normal circumstances. Someone had removed a bulb from the landing above and the hall and stairs were pitch dark.

But Emma's problems of perception were complicated by her eyes, and the booze. The most she could make out were outlines, the only light that cast into the hall from the faint glow in her own apartment. She was viewing Picasso—in the dark.

Then, a sound—a creak, very close. Someone was on the wood stairs and very close to her, almost at her landing.

"Mr. Cuchetto," she whispered.

Silence for a moment, then a whispered response:

"Yeah. It's all right. I took care of it. Go back to bed."

Emma tried to think.

Took care of what?

She closed her door, locked both locks.

Mr. Cuchetto?

How come she didn't catch the smell of his cigar?

But . . . there were other smells. One dominant. It was sharp, almost acrid. What was that? She had never smelled it before.

12

· · ·

Emma opened her eyes. Sunlight knifed into them, reminding her of how it felt when Dr. Pierce had first taken the bandages off.

She took quick note of the empty wine bottle on the floor, then closed her eyes.

It shut out the light, not the queasiness or the headache or . . .

Abruptly, she saw a mirror. In it, her face.

She turned over on the couch. She saw the wall clock: 3:48. She sat up on the couch.

She got up off the couch and stared in the mirror on the wall.

But there was nothing in the mirror . . . and then a face appeared . . .

A man. Pale, thin, his thin hair plastered to his head with sweat, his eyes black, yet alive—and scary.

His mouth was grotesque. Abnormally red lips.

And then he opened it and inside were small yellow teeth . . . and the mouth whispered at her but she couldn't hear what it said . . .

Then he shielded his face with a pale, trembling hand and . . .

Suddenly, the image collapsed and disappeared and Emma was staggering back to the couch, and she was aware she on the verge of screaming, her arms flailing. Ralph was barking violently.

She drew herself into a fetal position on the couch, not knowing what was coming next.

And then the face appeared again, and something hard surged in her and she lashed out at it, trying to drive it away, and then, abruptly as it had come, it was gone.

FOR A LONG time, Emma stayed on the couch, trying to hear anything coming from Valerie's apartment. Was she all right? What had happened?

Finally, she knew she had to know.

She got Ralph and they went out of the apartment and up the stairs as she gripped Ralph's harness tightly.

She put her ear to the door and listened awhile. No sound. She knocked.

No answer. She knocked harder.

Still no answer.

She was going to do it again, then realized that she wouldn't get an answer.

Why not?

Emma went down the stairs to the first floor, to Mr. Cuchetto's apartment, and knocked on the door. She knocked again.

"Mr. Cuchetto? Mr. Cuchetto!"

Where was he? He was always around. Why not now?

Suddenly, she felt the urge to be outside the building. She had to do something.

Outside, it was mild, almost subtropical for Chicago.

Faces on the street were blurred, then came into unfriendly focus.

She saw an old man who seemed to be scowling at her, a child on the other side of the street with a taunting expression, an old lady looking at her as if she were shit . . .

She closed her eyes, walked on. Maybe she was going crazy, she thought.

She had to do something. Now.

13

· · ·

TWENTY MINUTES AFTER SHE EXITED HER APART-
ment building, Emma was sitting at a desk in the
large bile-green squad room on the second floor of
the Third Precinct station house. Ralph was at her
side.

As usual, the sound of someone typing slowly—
it seemed all detectives went to one school where
single-finger typing was taught—was heard, and
there were other noises such as phones ringing
and chair wheels rolling, though it was hardly the
frenetic pace indicated by such TV shows as *Hill
Street Blues*.

Sitting behind the desk was a good-looking young
guy who was smoking, just as he had been when
Emma had arrived.

They were obviously not getting along.

"You're in the wrong place," said the detective,
whose name was Ridgely. "How'd you get up here?"

Indeed, he thought, later he would take a bite out of the desk sergeant's ass for letting a civilian get past him and up to the detectives' squad room.

"I took the stairs. Can you help me or not?"

"Just fill out the form, take it downstairs to the desk sergeant."

Emma looked at the sheet. It was a maze of lines and small print she couldn't begin to read.

"I can't."

Before he responded, a new voice was heard, this one deep, loud . . . and vaguely familiar to Emma.

"She's wearing a cross."

"Who?" Ridgely asked.

"The naked dead girl in the bathtub, Nina Getz. She's wearing a cross and her folks and her friends and the guy she was dating from English Lit say they've never seen it."

"Hallstrom, tour change has yet to commence. We just got here. Slow down. Ease up. Get off the sergeant's desk."

"The cross has got extra bars."

"So? What do you want me to do?" Ridgely said.

"How 'bout a little detecting?"

"I'd like to talk to Detective Hallstrom," Emma said as he left.

IN A SIDE office, Hallstrom had his head down, bent to the task, working—on a burrito, a not untypical homicide detective's meal for nine in the morning.

On the desk in front of him was an array of eight-by-ten photos. They were gruesome, explicit photos of a murdered woman. It was a measure of his experience that he could eat at all.

Emma Brody and Ralph loomed in his doorway.

"Detective Hallstrom?"

He looked up—and was shocked. He was John, the striptease artist from the bar, and standing in the doorway was the beautiful fiddler, the object of his naked affection.

He waited, somehow expecting recognition—and reproach—even though he knew she was blind. Maybe she'd recognize his voice . . .

"I'm eatin' my breakfast here."

Behind her, Barry appeared and, smiling broadly because he loved Hallstrom's discomfort, mimed a fiddler, sawing an imaginary bow over a violin.

Emma obviously was going nowhere. Hallstrom invited her to sit down—and tell her story.

FIVE MINUTES LATER, Emma had finished her story and on Hallstrom's face was a blend of bemusement—and disbelief.

"You're blind," he said.

"I was."

"You were . . . blind. Completely."

"Up till five or so weeks ago. Yes."

Hallstrom was now sure she didn't know him. The relationship was suddenly simpler.

"Okay, let me get this straight. You heard a guy in the hallway. You opened the door and looked out and spoke to him. That was last night, but you didn't see it until this morning."

"That's right."

"So, it's like . . . your eyes are driving the train and your brain's the caboose, it hasn't caught up yet."

"Something like that."

"Your eyes are having a delayed reaction?"

50

"It's a common occurrence with this type of surgery." Emma felt uncomfortable, defensive.

"Okay. How long were you blind?"

"Are there cops here," Emma said with an edge in her voice, "who work? Or do you all just sit around drinking coffee?"

"This is Homicide, lady. We never stop working." Hallstrom blinked. He was nettled. "Did you consume any alcoholic beverages last night?"

"You don't believe me."

"We can't go investigating every undigested turkey sandwich. Answer the question, did you have anything to drink?"

"Wine."

"How much?"

"A little. A lot. But it—"

"I can see seven dwarfs doing cartwheels on a little lot of wine. If you'll excuse me." Hallstrom waved her out of the room.

"Is there a fly in the room or are you asking me to leave?"

"Have a nice day, Miss Brody."

"There was someone in that hallway. I could smell him."

"What's it say on that?" Hallstrom pointed to a large poster on the bulletin board whose edges were curling. It said, "DETECTIVES DO IT UNDER-COVER."

Emma squinted, but couldn't read it.

"Fuck you, Hallstrom."

"Whoa, whoa, whoa, that will not be necessary. Maybe other people cut you slack 'cause you're blind . . ."

"I don't want *slack*."

51

Hallstrom jumped up and thumped the poster with a fist.

"That's not five feet away from you. You can't see, lady."

"You smoke. You use Coast deodorant soap," Emma said flatly. "The yellow one. You take cream in your coffee. There's eggs, chorizo, tomatoes, and cilantro in that thing you were eating, and the gum you're chewing is spearmint."

"You do that trick at parties?"

Emma got up, pushing her chair behind her hard. Ralph stood up with her.

"Look," he said, "we'll send a car by."

He went around and stopped in the doorway. "Hey, uh, Miss Brody."

"What?"

Hallstrom wanted to say something else. "Cute dog," he said.

"He bites," Emma shot back.

She turned to go, and what he really had on his mind surged out. "Why'd you ask for me?"

"I liked the sound of your voice."

Hallstrom looked at her—and wondered if she were playing with him.

Then she was gone.

A FEW HOURS later, Emma sat in an examining chair. Dr. Pierce was looking at her corneas with a slit lamp. But he sensed that she was seeing him for another reason, because of what she'd just told him.

"How are they doing?" he asked.

"Awful. My head is always splitting."

"I can give you something—"

"The guy was not a dream. It was real."

52

"The police are checking into it, right?"

"People treat me like a cripple."

"The guy was an asshole."

"He made me feel like an idiot. I never used to care what people thought of me."

"Are you saying how other people see you is . . . actually what you are?"

"The last time I looked I was a little girl and then I—I . . . I blink, and . . ."

Emma was close to tears. The detective had upset her, but it went much deeper than that. She felt herself in some sort of tailspin.

"I look like my mother. I look like her."

Pierce's face softened. He took her hands in his. "You're not her. You're not what the cop thinks. You're . . . very attractive. Don't you see that? Don't you see anything beautiful?"

"Music is beautiful. The things I *see*," she said slowly, painfully, "they just make my head ache . . . my heart."

"Be glad. Most people are entirely numb by the time they reach your age."

"I'd like to be numb for a while," Emma said.

Pierce squeezed her hands. "No, you wouldn't Emma. Believe me, you wouldn't."

14
· · ·

JOHN HALLSTROM HAD HAD VERY LITTLE SLEEP over the previous forty-eight hours. He'd had to handle a bar killing of a black, a vehicular homicide, and a gay killing, the last particularly and typically a bloodbath, the victim stabbed over a hundred times.

All not only required lots of paperwork but lots of investigative work—right away. Hallstrom had always believed the cliché that if you didn't solve a homicide in the first seventy-two hours it went into the realm of the whodunnit, a far more difficult prospect.

But since he'd taken the squeals—answered the complaints—he was required to attend the post, or autopsy—or canoe-making, as the cops referred to it—of all three victims. That had been boring in the extreme, the only jolly moment provided when a young patrolman, attending perhaps his third autopsy, had had to witness Hallstrom eating a jelly donut while one man was being done. Hallstrom, of course, had squeezed some jelly out of the donut and licked it off just as the ME was lifting the dripping, shiny heart out of the chest. The young cop had turned light green.

But Hallstrom was not about to get any sleep soon. At around midnight—when he should still be with the soft young woman he was with when he'd received the emergency call—he found himself at another scene— a scene that would have made even some experienced detectives turn light green.

The deceased was in the bathroom. The room was ripe and the body showed extensive lividity. The victim, a white female, had been there awhile.

She was in a tub half filled with what looked like blood.

One hand was draped over the ledge on one side, another rested on the other ledge. Blood had dripped down from both wrists, which had been slit. There were bruises on her neck.

Around her neck was a small cross with double bars.

"Sorry to fuck up your date," Barry said as they viewed the scene, a photographer busily snapping pictures.

"Yeah. I told her to wait for me. Relax in a nice hot bath."

Ridgely shook his head, his brow knit. "This ain't no crackhead, John. This girl's got folks. Name's Valerie Wheaton. The super, Cuchetto, found her when her boss called, worried. She hadn't shown up for two days. Offender accessed apartment through the fire-escape window. There was a struggle in the front room . . . he strangled her. Raped her. Or raped and strangled her."

"That's a lot of assumptions, Tom."

"Looks like semen flaking off the carpet out there. Pile is crushed all the way to here, like he dragged her postmortem."

"Guess she and Nina Getz found God in the same jewelry box," Hallstrom said.

Hallstrom bent down and took a pen from his jacket pocket. He removed the cross and held it dangling. Light reflected off it.

"Who," he almost whispered to the victim, "are you supposed to be? Who does he want you to be?"

He stood up.

"Why," Ridgely asked, "does he slit their wrists after they're dead?"

"Because he's suicidal? Because his mother's suicidal? This ain't no slit. He practically cut her hands off . . . I guess a knife or a straight razor."

Hallstrom tapped the pen on one of the victim's fingernails. "Let's just hope she scratched a good chunk out of him before she went down."

He stood up.

"Help them remove the body. I'm gonna do the neighbors."

Hallstrom made his way slowly through Valerie Wheaton's apartment. Her life-style hung on the walls, posters and pictures of everything from the Rolling Stones in their heyday to the grave of Jim Morrison.

Hallstrom heard the sound before he opened the front door, and then it filled the hall: the music of

a violin, mournful and stark, filling the building—
with sadness.

Hallstrom knew exactly where the sound was coming from, and who was making it.

15

· · ·

Hallstrom knocked on the door where the music was coming from, and the playing stopped. Fifteen seconds later Emma was standing in the doorway.

The sight of her triggered memories of their meeting—or clash—at the precinct, and pointed up the embarrassment that had been building in Hallstrom since he'd realized that the victim upstairs was the very person she had been talking about.

Now he set his jaw, hoping that his eyes wouldn't give him away.

"She's dead," Emma said flatly, and might have added, "Right?" but didn't. It was a statement of cold, hard, sad fact.

"Yes, yes, she is. Can I come in . . . ask you a few questions?"

Emma turned and walked away, leaving the door ajar. Hallstrom walked into the apartment . . . and got something of a shock.

It was, he thought, like going into a church where the lights weren't working. Illumination was from one source: small candles, which permeated the place with a waxy smell. In the dimness, Hallstrom was having a hard time seeing.

He looked at Emma. Her eyes seemed more lively tonight, more focused than when they'd met at the station house. In fact, they were not unfriendly.

Hallstrom responded in kind. "What's with the candles? You expecting someone?"

"It's easier on my eyes. I can turn on the light."

"It's okay." He fished a notebook from a rear pocket. "Anything you can tell me about Valerie Wheaton?"

"I never really spoke to her. The only thing I really know is . . . she took the stairs two at a time and she was . . . well . . . she was a very noisy lover."

"Noisy, huh? Did she have a boyfriend that you know of?"

"Yes, she did."

"And was this one guy, or did she see a lotta guys."

"It was one guy."

"How did you know it was one guy?"

"I could hear him."

"You saw this guy's face. He saw you. Okay. Can you go over one more time for me exactly what happened when you opened the door that night?"

"I looked out. I couldn't really see anyone, because . . ."

"Your operation, right."

"But I heard breathing. So I said, 'Mr. Cuchetto.' "

"And he said, 'Yes.' But it wasn't Cuchetto, because Cuchetto says he was sleeping, and his wife verifies that. So tell me every word this guy says."

" 'Yes. It's all right. I took care of it. Go back to bed.' "

"How long have you lived here?"

"Almost five years."

"You've lived here five years but didn't recognize that it wasn't the building manager's voice."

"He whispered."

"I'm gonna have to ask you to come down to the station. We'll do up a sketch, you'll look at some pictures."

"Tonight?"

"Yeah, how's your vision? Can you see me clearly now?"

"Detectives do it undercover," Emma said.

"That's, uh . . . that's the flashback thing."

"Is that a reference to police work, or fucking?"

"It's a dick joke."

"A dick joke."

"Dick. Detectives. You know. Dick Tracy. We call ourselves dicks."

"I see."

"With good reason, you're probably saying. So here's my card, and I'm going to put my beeper number on the back. If you remember anything after tonight, call, anytime. It's a twenty-four-hour beeper."

She reached out to take the card—and missed it.

"God, I hate this," she said.

With his other hand, Hallstrom took hers. Noticing the soft skin and delicate bones, he pressed the card into her palm.

He looked to meet her eyes, but they were closed.

Then she opened them.

"You like flowers?" she asked.

"Flowers?"

"Soft skin for a man. Smells like that lotion that they make out of roses."

"The wind. Stings your hands."

Emma paused before she spoke. She remembered something about the night Valerie was murdered.

"The guy on the stairs. He had a weird smell."

"He smelled bad?"

"Not bad."

"What did he smell like?"

"Sweat. Soap. Very strong ... strange soap. Uh ... grease."

"Like cooking."

"Like cars."

"Sweat, soap, grease. That it on the smells?"

Emma paused again. It looked to Hallstrom as if she were fighting to remember something.

"There was something ..." she said. "I don't know ... very vague ... I could be imagining it ..."

"Tell me."

"There were seven little men behind him doing cartwheels."

"Is that a fact. You wanna get your coat?"

16

· · ·

FIFTEEN MINUTES AFTER THEY ARRIVED AT THE precinct, Emma was brought to a large windowed room with a big table on which was arrayed a large number of mug-shot books. She started looking at them, a female officer nearby assisting her.

A few minutes after Emma started looking at the pictures, the Homicide commander, Detective Sergeant Mitchell, approached Hallstrom and Ridgely, who were standing in the squad room next to the room where Emma was.

Mitchell asked them to fill him in.

"We got skin cells under her fingernails," Ridgely said. A few minutes earlier one of the forensics guys at the scene had phoned in this detail.

"That's six weeks in the lab," Mitchell said.

"We'll only wait," Hallstrom said, "for the DNA on the blood type. Semen on the swabs and on the carpet."

"We got the boyfriend outta bed," Ridgely said, referring to Valerie Wheaton's boyfriend. "He's in there weeping up a storm. But he has an alibi that checks out. Killer was wearing gloves, we got no prints so far."

They were interrupted by the female cop, who had just come out of the room where Emma was poring over the photos.

"She can't see the mug shots."

"I'll get a magnifying glass," Ridgely said.

Ridgely left. Mitchell looked at Hallstrom. "What do you think? A serial?"

"If he is, he's just getting started. We cross-referenced his M.O. . . . the cross, the wrists, the bathtub . . . with the national computer . . . nothing. Which means he's probably not a drifter. And if he lives here, we'll catch him."

Hallstrom looked through the window at Emma in the other room. "We have an eyewitness."

"She couldn't even fill out a report."

"She's got a vision problem, but I think she's for real. She checks out. So far."

"Jury isn't going to see how her tits fall out when she plays the violin."

"That's low. Low and cheap. Is that how a sergeant talks?"

"One thing at a time. You're off the chart. Hand your other cases to Barry."

"All of 'em. My gimme? My one fuckin' bunt in a year and a half," Hallstrom said, referring to the killing of the black guy, which he was on the verge of solving. "I've almost cleared it and you want me to give it to Barry? He can't find his ass in his swimsuit."

"From now on you got one case. Put it to bed, John. Quick. Your witness isn't enough. She's too shaky. Get more. Nail him. Don't let this thing grow. Don't let them write a book about this guy."

"That was good," Hallstrom said.

"I'm getting the hang of it?"

"You'll be fuckin' mayor by forty."

EMMA'S TREK THROUGH the mug-shot books, aided by a magnifying glass, had been unsuccessful. But then she had been interviewed by the police artist, who had spent a half hour trying to get a description out of Emma that they could render into a usable sketch which they could distribute.

The entire process gave Emma a headache, first of all because she had not seen much of anything on the stairs that night, and second of all because she wasn't sure whether what she was recalling was an actual memory or some sort of hallucination.

But an hour after the artist started to interview her, the computer the artist was working with rolled out a sketch.

Emma looked at it.

To be sure, it was a frightening picture, but it was not the yellow-toothed red-lipped monster of her dreams . . . nor was it exactly right. Something was missing, but she could not think of what.

"I don't know," Emma said.

"We'll go for it for now," Hallstrom said. "Thank you, Ms. Brody. You've been a tremendous help." He paused. He eyed Emma carefully. "You're not worried, are you? About this guy . . . coming back?"

"He thought I was blind. I looked right at him and asked him if he was someone else."

"Right. Okay, I'll run this down to printing."

Hallstrom took the sketch, went out the door, then came back. "You're free to go. Miss Brody."

"Yes, master," Emma said.

TIRED, THE HEADACHE still there, Emma returned to her building and started to wearily climb the stairs.

Then she looked up, and froze.

Valerie Wheaton was on the top on the landing, making a face at her.

Emma blinked.

Valerie went away, and in her place was a cop, dusting for prints on the railing.

Emma couldn't wait to get in her apartment.

17

· · ·

THE DAY AFTER SHE'D TRIED TO "MAKE" THE PERSON she had seen in the hall, Emma was on the street in downtown Chicago, Ralph at her side. Candice Archer was busily stapling posters to a telephone pole. The posters announced that the band, the Drovers, would appear at the Cabaret Metro. Emma was acting as poster bearer.

The sky was gray, the wind chill. It seemed appropriate, Candice thought, to what she was sensing was going on inside Emma.

"What's up, Emma?"

Emma did not answer.

But Candice knew what was up. "The girl died. There's nothing you could have done."

Emma paused, then answered. "Candice, if there's something beautiful in this windy fuckin' city, I would like to see it."

THAT NIGHT, EMMA and Candice sat in Chicago Stadium and observed what could truly be described as poetry in motion . . . Michael Jordan sailing through the air to slam-dunk as a Charlotte Hornet tried vainly to stop him.

Candice's eyes were trained on Jordan with something approaching demonic intensity.

"His skin. The sweat on his skin, you just want to run your hand along those muscles," she said.

"Is he wearing the suit?"

"Huh?"

"Is he wearing the uniform in your jerk-off fantasy."

"Women don't jerk off."

"What? They rub off."

"Of course, blind women, that's a whole other story."

"What story is that?"

"I just want to know . . . what it's like."

"Put a bag over your head."

"Come on . . ."

Emma grew serious. "I never got nervous around men. I just . . . pulled them in . . . to my fantasy. And I was in control. I mean, in my head these men could really be anybody. Now I see them. And it scares me. The *sight* of a man who . . . excites me makes me . . . terribly awkward."

Candice's eyes followed the power, speed, and symmetry of a Bulls fast break. "Men are beautiful, aren't they?"

"And they know it. This cop really pours it on. He understands, he's sensitive, he's funny. But when he gets his information, wham, next witness."

Candice had her own concern. "You gonna play Cabaret Metro Saturday?"

"I'm nervous. I've never actually seen an audience . . ."

"Put a bag over your head."

"This cop is so . . . edgy. He's not comfortable . . . in the suit. He doesn't wear it. It just contains him."

"Is he wearing the suit?"

"Huh?"

"In your jerk-off fantasy?"

"Shut up," Emma said.

Candice smiled broadly, then watched another Bulls fast break.

"Men are beautiful, aren't they?" she said.

EMMA GOT BACK from the game at around midnight, and immediately went into the bedroom and emptied the contents of a small bag onto the bed.

She smiled, even though the items—mascara, blush, lipstick, and other makeup essentials—made her nervous. It had been years since she had handled anything like this, and the last time she had it had been her mother's . . . and the results of that had been horrendous.

But that was then, this is now, she thought, and she manipulated the lipstick until a pale bronze stick emerged. Then she looked at the mirror on the back of the closet door, and the backs of her upper arms flashed with gooseflesh: Her mother was looking at her.

She turned her head down and away. She wanted to look again, but couldn't.

She stood up, turned, and then abruptly stripped

the blanket off the bed and threw it, still without looking, over the closet door so it covered the mirror.

Only then did she look. She was shaking.

18

· ‑ ·

RIDGELY, BARRY, AND NED CONGREGATED AROUND the coffee machine—or whatever it was it produced—and talked, naturally, about murder.

All of them agreed that it was quite obvious now that a serial murderer was at work. One giveaway was that he had a pattern, and left the scene in a certain way. More, the M.O. was fetishistic, ritualistic: Something was going on in his head that compelled him to leave each of his murder victims a certain way. Nina Getz and Valerie Wheaton had been strangled and had had their wrists carefully cut, and a silver cross had been left in a prominent place.

The puzzling thing was to find a common thread among the victims. Serial killers invariably would home in on victims who shared common physical characteristics. For example, Ted Bundy, who'd killed about forty women in the seventies and eighties, zeroed in on young, pretty women with longish dark hair. Chicago's own John Wayne Gacy's thirty-odd victims were all small, muscular young men in their late teens. Hillside Strangler Steven Bianchi killed prostitutes.

Speaking of pretty women, Ned mentioned that Emma Brody had been in.

"She was in, the fiddler?" Barry said. That, he thought, would be the second time.

"It was her," Ned confirmed, "the same one."

Abruptly, Hallstrom appeared and the conversation, which might have continued about Emma, came to an abrupt halt.

Hallstrom carried a bag with him. He also had a fatigued expression on his face.

He went over to a desk and dumped the contents of the bag on the desk. Fifty or so little boxes spewed out, some of them opening in the process and spilling out their contents—silver Byzantine crosses.

Ridgely knew that this was the result of Hallstrom's trying to do a trace on the crosses found on Getz and Wheaton, but he couldn't resist a one-liner. "I think God already gave up on you."

"This model is like the Honda of Byzantine crosses. Four churches carry it in their little gift shops. There's even a fuckin' catalogue. He could have gotten them anywhere."

Ned pushed Ridgely towards Hallstrom. Ridgely pulled a letter out of his jacket pocket.

"Someone fucked up," Ridgely said. "We got one of the fiddler's letters with Valerie Wheaton's mail."

"So?" Hallstrom said.

"So take it over to her," Barry said.

71

"We'll each throw in a hundred if you sink the torpedo."

"No way, guys. Not this time."

"Oh, bullshit," Ned said.

"I'm serious here. By the book." He smiled. "Why waste this body on a chick who can't see it?"

AS WITH THE other cops, the case was inside Hallstrom totally, and most of his waking hours were spent thinking about it, trying to establish some sort of link, connection, between the various parts that would enable him to make that giant link—to make a suspect.

He went into his office, took off his jacket, and hung it up. He took the letter from his coat pocket and sat down at his desk.

He looked at it, letting his mind free-float over the facts of the case, hoping the letter, which did not seem to have any significance at all, would nevertheless trigger something.

But after a while he realized the letter wasn't going to trigger anything—not tonight.

He got up and used a thumbtack to secure it to the only space available on his bulletin board—on top of the "DETECTIVES DO IT UNDERCOVER" poster.

He thought of the fiddler. She was a beautiful woman, and he certainly would not object to doing it undercover—or overcover—with her.

And somehow, something deep in his gut told him that she was at the center of it all . . . not just that she had seen the perp, but . . . he couldn't come up with anything.

He felt a little chill. Should he put someone with her?

He sensed she was too independent for that. And she had likely been right. Why would a killer be afraid of being ID'd by a blind woman? He wouldn't, right?

19

• • •

EMMA DIDN'T GIVE A SHIT. OR AT LEAST, THAT'S what she was telling herself.

When she arrived at the Cabaret Metro there was a line halfway around the block. She immediately felt a surge of anxiety. It had been weeks since she had played in front of an audience.

Now, she waited in the wings with the other band members, ready to go on in a few minutes. On, she knew, to a packed house.

One of the other band members, Sean, must have read the fear and doubt in her face.

He walked over and took her hand.

"You'll be great," he said.

A moment later, Emma heard a little commotion and turned. It was Candice, beaming, clutching a newspaper in her hand.

"Sold out," she said, belaboring the obvious. "It must be the *Sun-Times*. The write-up."

From the stage area, there had been the consistent murmuring sound of a crowd. Now the public address system boomed, and the crowd quieted—and Emma's heart rate increased.

"The Cabaret Metro is proud to present, the Drovers!"

Emma's mind churned, fearful of not being able to see or perform or maybe hallucinating or . . .

From behind her back, Candice produced a paper bag, held it towards Emma, and rattled it.

"Last chance," she said.

"You keep it," Emma said. "You need it more than I do."

Sean took her hand again as the band started onto the stage. And the last thing Emma thought was that whatever was out there, it couldn't be worse than what she had already experienced. Of that she was sure.

If she had any doubt about her ability to see, it was answered immediately. The stage lights blinded her, and she held up her hand to shield her eyes, a gesture she had not made in twenty years.

It was scary and satisfying at the same time. Slowly, her eyes started to adjust, and then she became aware of the applause—thunderous applause—and she wondered what the crowd looked like, and then suddenly, there it was: hundreds of faces turned towards her, hands coming together almost violently. It was the first time in her life that she had faced an audience that she could see.

Then the satisfaction started to fade and what was left was the fear. She was aware that she was clutching the fiddle fiercely, too tightly, threatening to crack it.

All these people, she knew, were looking at her: Emma, the miracle of modern science, the blind girl who could see again. Bette Davis, move over.

Then she felt a hand, the steadying hand of Sean. He pulled her forward and she realized she was not on her mark. She was just standing there, a blob.

The light, the sound, the sight of it was all too much. She closed her eyes, and darkness—but not as complete as before—enveloped and protected her.

It's better, she thought. Maybe it will be better.

Gracefully she tucked the violin under her chin and waited.

The mournful, plaintive cry of bagpipes was heard. Emma raised her arm, ready to stroke, ready to enter a new life . . .

Just as her cue came there was a shrill catcall from the crowd, and she brought the bow across the strings and a cacophonous sound emerged: It sounded more like a power tool with motor trouble than a violin.

She opened her eyes, scanned the crowd. Now, bastard, where are you?

But it was just a sea of faces, and as she waited for her cue again, she scanned them individually as much as she could.

And the faces looked at her . . .

Then, just a moment before her cue, she saw another face and her stomach lurched and hollowed.

Oh, Jesus Christ! Jesus Christ.

All sound had stopped, all noise: There, the reflections of the stage lights eerily throwing his face into sharp planes, unmoving, staring at her, was the face she'd seen in the hall. The face of the killer—and he was looking directly at her.

For a moment, she was transfixed, and then she started to move off the stage, stumbling, half running, a small animal in sheer panic in the open, running for its life, with a predator waiting that did not yet need to run, knowing it would make a meal of the prey whenever it wished.

Behind, as in a dream, she heard noise. The band was playing, going on without her.

Her face was almost pure white as she ran into Candice, almost knocking her down.

She was not sure she could talk.

"Call Detective Hallstrom," she said in a throaty whisper. "Call him!"

20

...

Less than fifteen minutes later, a horde of black-and-whites had arrived at the club, and then so had Hallstrom.

Emma had given him a description of the killer— or her perception of the killer—and then Hallstrom had gotten it out onto the wire.

Inside the bar now, Hallstrom, Ridgely, and other dicks worked the waitresses, bartenders, and other club personnel trying to get a detailed description of the person Emma saw. Backstage, Emma and the band packed up. It was impossible to go on after the disruption.

Emma felt that all she wanted to do was run— and keep running.

There was a long, uncomfortable silence. Then Sean spoke. "You can't let this man stop you living your life, Emma. He probably wasn't even there."

"What?"

"You may have seen someone who looked like him," Candice said.

"You think I'm faking this? You think I imagined it?"

"No, I . . ." Candice said.

A melange of images assaulted Emma—of Candice in the hospital, of Candice pushing her to get out, or Candice pushing her to spill her guts to the *Sun-Times* reporter, of Candice pushing, pushing, pushing. And for who?

"What else do you think I'm imagining, huh? That girl's dead body coming down the stairs past my door in a stretcher?"

"Just forget it."

"You wish I hadn't seen him. 'Cause you'd be off the hook. If you hadn't set up that article, Candice, if you hadn't plastered those flyers with my picture on every street in the city . . . that's why he was here. We should have stopped it."

"You're not the only person in the band," Candice countered. "That article was about all of us."

"Us? You're not in the band. You're not in the band. You're not the manager. You're not the publicist. You're Michael's girlfriend."

Candice was going to answer—but couldn't. Emma stalked out of the room.

FIVE MINUTES LATER, Emma was sitting on a box she had found in the alley adjacent to the side entrance to the club. Ralph circled, nuzzling her as if he knew the chaotic state she was in, and tried to comfort her.

She glanced to her left as the stage door was opened—and John Hallstrom came out. He was a reassuring sight.

He came up to her. "Are you all right?"

"Did you find him?"

"We picked up some guys loitering in the neighborhood that could fit the drawing. We need you to come down to the station for a lineup."

"Can we drop Ralph at home?"

"We'll use the siren."

As he drove, Hallstrom reached into his pocket and produced a bar of soap.

He handed it to Emma.

She sniffed it, then shook her head no. It was not the soap she'd smelled.

Then they were silent and Emma was rigid, but Hallstrom noticed something else—an air of almost wistfulness about her, as if she were somewhere else.

"Ever hear of Tir Na Nog?" Emma said.

"Some magical place where the leprechauns hang? With the roilling hills and the . . ."

" . . . colorful skies. You Irish?"

"Half," Hallstrom said.

"I thought you were. I thought the world would be like Tir Na Nog. If I ever finally saw it again. It's been very disappointing."

She looked at him, her face suffused with sadness.

"That's all crap, you know. Promised lands. Prince Charming," he said.

"I didn't say anything about Prince Charming."

"Good, 'cause no one can live up to princely and charming."

"Is that why you don't have anyone in your life?"

Hallstrom felt himself get a little hot. If someone else had said that he might have replied: The truth hurts. But he didn't. "What makes you think I don't have anyone in my life?"

"You keep strange hours."

"You ask personal questions."

"What other kind are there?"

Hallstrom still simmered a bit. "This is all you need to know about me. I carry a badge, I could put on some weight, I spend too many nights in back alleys."

"What you see is what you get."

"Exactly."

"Got to be more than that. Six weeks ago I wouldn't have been able to see you."

21

· · ·

An hour after they spoke in the alley, Hallstrom and Emma arrived at the station house to view the lineup. Emma was glad to be with Hallstrom. She liked his sheer physical presence, and also the plain fact that he was with her and could protect her. Since the incident her stomach had felt the consistency of Jell-O. It was still very much that way when they went into the station house.

Emma and Hallstrom were met there by Mitchell and Ridgely, and the detectives accompanied her to the room where she was to view the people who resembled the man she had described to Hallstrom.

They led her to a room where there was a large picture window that looked into another room with a stage, the back wall of which contained a height chart.

It was explained to her by Hallstrom that the

suspect side of the glass was mirrored. She couldn't be seen.

Emma was glad she would be physically isolated from the people.

Suspects started to file onto the stage from an adjacent room, stopped, turned, and faced in Emma's direction.

Emma looked—and her stomach lurched. Since the operation, she might describe her regained sight as intermittent, ranging from pretty good to terrible. Now, while not terrible, it was not that good.

The problem was that the people on the stage facing her all looked the same, sort of like mannequins. There were no distinguishing features to isolate one from the other.

She strained to see. She was aware that her credibility as an eyewitness was in question. She was also aware that her safety could depend on her being able to identify someone.

She tried harder, but still could not see.

Then the men who had been facing her were commanded by a voice on a PA system to turn so she could view their profiles, though she wondered how this could help. She wasn't able to distinguish anyone straight on. Why would a profile view help?

It didn't. She could not see anyone . . . and she almost desperately wanted to.

Then the men turned face front again, and the killer looked at her. Right at her. Through her.

"Number six," she said, her heart hammering.

Then she blinked and the image was gone, his body dissolving, going out of focus—into someone else she couldn't recognize.

God.

"No," Emma said, "maybe I . . ."

Mitchell gave Hallstrom a what-the-hell's-going-on look, and so did Ridgely. It was a question Hallstrom was asking himself.

Emma stared, rubbed her eyes, changed her position, even shielded her eyes, but Number 6 still remained the person he had transformed into.

Silently, the group in the viewing room broke up, and the last thing Emma heard was the voice on the PA telling the people in the lineup to file off the stage.

"I THOUGHT," HALLSTROM said, almost bitterly, "you said your eyes were getting better."

He was escorting her out of the building, and he opened the front door with a sort of shove, another indication of how he was feeling, which in a phrase was pissed off.

"They were, they are," Emma said, an edge to her voice.

Hallstrom made no comment until they were on the street. "How better are they?"

"It's been a rough fucking night, Hallstrom."

"Can you read? Can you tell time? Can you walk down the street without a dog leading the way?"

"Can you walk down the street with that bug up your ass?"

Hallstrom paused before speaking. "How," he asked, "were you blinded?"

"What?"

"How were you blinded in the first place?"

" . . . my mother . . ."

"Your *mother*," Hallstrom said. He seemed not to want to listen, just to hurt.

84

"None of your business," Emma snapped.

"Your mother blinded you. That must have contributed to your mental health."

"What the hell does that mean?"

Hallstrom stopped walking. His voice dripped with sarcasm. "Number six? In the lineup. He was a uniform . . . on a stakeout across town the night of the murder. You ID'd a cop as the murderer."

"Don't people make mistakes? Normal sighted people. Maybe he wasn't even there."

"I never said that."

"In the lineup! Maybe you blew it, Hallstrom. Maybe you let him slip through your fingers."

Hallstrom grimaced. "We get this all the time at the precinct. I saw a robbery, I saw a murder, I saw Elvis Presley at my brother's bar mitzvah."

"Crazy people," Emma said flatly. "That's what you're talking about."

"Lonely people," Hallstrom cut in, "people who like attention . . ."

"People who like attention . . ."

"Look there's the killer! No, it's a light post."

Emma cut in. "Like people who strip naked and shake their ass in a bar full of people?"

Hallstrom stopped, looked at Emma. A little blood drained from his face. "You saw me?" he said.

"I didn't. The guys in the band recognized you."

Hallstrom laughed a little. "Things are not what they seem."

"What?" Emma said.

"Little secret detective credo I have. 'Tell me not, in mournful numbers/Life is but an empty dream/For the soul is dead that slumbers/And things are not what they seem.'"

"Oh, brother. Closet poet cop quoting Longfellow. You are really something."

"I just use it to pick up women."

"I bet it works."

"Not as well as my handcuffs."

They laughed.

"You're the first in a long time," Hallstrom continued, "to know what it is. Most of the women I go out with think it's an old song by Guns 'n' Roses."

"I don't know your first name."

"John."

"Wanna get some coffee . . . John?"

22
. . .

JOHN HALLSTROM FELT LIKE A FISH OUT OF WATER.
Emma felt at home. And she had calmed down
considerably.

They were sitting at a small battered table in
the corner of a small battered room that was the
Artists Coffee House on Weller Street, in the Old
Town section of the city.

The room contained perhaps a dozen tables, maybe half occupied. From the look and feel of the room,
and the people, Hallstrom sensed he might be in the
psycho ward at Cooks County Hospital.

Their order was taken by a waiter who sported
a red bandanna wrapped around his neck, tight
pants, a lisp, and a shaved head. For a moment,
Hallstrom thought he recognized him as someone
he'd once collared on a morals charge.

Hallstrom wanted regular coffee, but that was
not to be. Espresso was as close as he could get.

He spoke when the waiter—or perpetrator—left.

"Who are these people?" he asked.

"Songwriters, musicians . . ."

Hallstrom nodded. "You, uh, you write the lyrics for the band?"

"No, I've tried. But Michael does most of it."

For a moment, Hallstrom was preoccupied with the sight of an older guy with a goatee and brown cigarette talking with a woman who looked a minimum of a thousand years old and had last washed her hair about eight hundred years earlier.

"What do you think," he said, nodding towards them, "he's talking about?"

"He's trying to find a rhyme for 'pretentious.' "

"Park benches."

"Very good. Wanna write me some lyrics?"

"Wanna catch a murderer?"

"Okay," Emma said, and thought that it was amazing that she could be so calm. She shouldn't be. She should still feel like a bowl of Jell-O. But an hour with Hallstrom was just the medicine she needed.

"Okay," Hallstrom said.

They looked at each other, almost as if in a hockey face-off, or a jump ball in basketball—the beginning of some kind of competition.

Emma smiled. "One, two, three, *go!*"

"There once was a man from Nantucket . . ." Hallstrom said.

Emma's face was suddenly flat, serious. "He doesn't like blood," she said.

Hallstrom's eyes narrowed. That observation flew in the face of certain facts. Chiefly one.

"He slits their wrists," he said.

"That's the last thing he does, and he scrubs his hands so raw I could smell them, then he gets out. He doesn't want to see them bleed."

"Good. Why?"

"You tell me."

"His kill is clean. So she can be nice and pretty while he . . ." Hallstrom's voice trailed off. He did not want to offend her.

"Does it rhyme with Nantucket?"

The waiter brought their espressos and sashayed away.

Hallstrom sipped his, and grimaced. Then he set the cup down.

"He doesn't hate her," he said. "It's not rape. He loves her. But she won't sit still, right? A rapist, he gets off on that. He likes a live one, the look in her eyes when the knife shows up. But this guy just wants a body. A blow-up doll that won't fly out the window if you squeeze too hard. He stops it kicking. He dresses it up. Like her. Like the one who wore the cross. He gets his little bit of heaven, then he slits her wrists . . . to make sure she never goes back. To being what she was. Long live his baby. Pickled in her own juices."

"You're good at that."

"My job is the only thing I'm good at."

"I doubt it. A man who smells like roses . . ." She touched his hand.

"It's just to cover the scent of blood."

Emma took her hand away, the feel of his flesh lingering. "You think you'll catch him?"

"Yeah," Hallstrom said, "you saw him."

"Thanks," Emma said.

"Then we'll catch him."

23

· · ·

BEFORE HALLSTROM DROPPED EMMA OFF, HE SUG-
gested that he place someone with her for protection, but she declined. "I've been used to taking care
of myself my whole life," she said. "I can do it now."

In fact, she sensed she was being unreasonable—
but still declined. Maybe being rejected and abused
by your mother made you defiant, dependent on
yourself—because you sensed there was no one else.

Unable to change her mind, he warned her to be
very careful, that she should not get herself in any
situation where she was isolated, where a killer
could corner her. More, she might consider carrying
Mace—or paint remover in a spray can—to provide
a welcome for anyone who might try to attack her.
He also told her to make sure that her doors and
windows were locked, and to call him if she felt a
need—she had his beeper number—or 911 if necessary. Above all, he said, don't take any chances.

Emma was touched and warmed by his concern, and for the next two days was very careful, keeping alert. She carried a small can of hair spray in her pocketbook. That could discourage people too.

On the evening of the second day, she went to see Dr. Pierce on a regular appointment at his office at the hospital. She hoped that she would do well.

Shortly after she arrived he had her sitting in a chair, looking across the other side of the room at an eye chart, with a special light playing on it.

Over her eyes she held a black, masklike tool called an occluder. "T, P, H."

Pierce was pleased.

"That's okay. How about this?" he said.

"M . . . L . . . U . . . Whose eyes are these anyway? They can't see."

"Miss Brody, those are the corneas of two healthy girls in their early twenties."

"Really? Who?"

"I've been waiting for that one. I know a little about one of the donors. The family wrote to me."

"How did they find you?"

"Sometimes I think these people have a right to know their daughter's death had some good in it. Try this line."

"N, Q, U, E, B, T, 2."

"Good."

"If only the whole world was separated into still squares of light."

EMMA HAD ONCE told Pierce about the man in the hallway, and now he offered to accompany her home. She declined, telling him that she was being careful and—the same thing she had told Hallstrom—that she could take care of herself.

And she agreed with what Sean from the band had told her: Don't let anyone—even a killer—run your life. She was trying to do that, without being foolish.

After the examination, Pierce walked with her down the hospital corridor. As they did, the thought of the donor surfaced again in Emma's mind.

"How did she die?"

"Auto accident."

"Can I meet them? Her family?"

"That's not a good idea."

"Don't they want to meet me?"

"Yes, but . . ."

"Then what's the problem?"

"Emma, you have to move on. Repair your life. And so do they. Don't prolong their grief."

"You're just like John. You both have to wait till someone dies before you can go to work."

"John?"

"Detective Hallstrom."

"You saw him again?"

"I had a little panic in the club last night."

"Are you all right?"

"I can't seem to get the old touch back."

"Would you like me to come some night? Maybe I could . . . help . . . somehow. What is it you've been seeing?"

They turned a corner and Emma did not have a chance to answer: The killer was standing at the end of the hall, dressed in the greens of an orderly.

She stopped, rubbed her eyes.

"What?" Pierce said, puzzled.

Then, the image evaporated. Emma rubbed her eyes.

"Nothing. Ralph's parked on level two," she said, referring to the parking garage. Christ, hallucinating horror was getting to be old hat.

"Aren't you supposed to give him to another blind person?"

"He's too old. He gets to retire. Lucky for me."

"Call me . . . anytime," Pierce said, and peeled off down a corridor going in the opposite direction from Emma.

THE PARKING GARAGE was connected to the hospital. It was a typical garage—massive concrete slabs and pillars, a ramp that wound to a roof parking area, elevators, stairs—and it was never empty, though at certain times of day, as now, it was only about one quarter full.

And it was just the place Hallstrom wouldn't want her in.

She knew what he would say: Don't go in alone . . . this is the kind of situation you don't want to get into.

But Emma chose to go in. She knew, vaguely, that it was important not to let the fear beat her—Sean was right about that. If she had let her fears beat her, she wouldn't be alive.

And again, she was just plain defiant.

She stepped on the elevator that would take her to the garage.

24
• • •

Emma had made a deal with the attendant in the small booth on the second level to watch Ralph until she came back, and Ralph was raring to go when she got there. The attendant, a young, swarthy guy, did not speak much English, but he knew how to smile, and smiled broadly when Emma produced the ten for Ralph's release.

She started back across the garage, and was feeling much less jumpy than on the trip to the booth. Then she had seemed to be hearing and seeing things in the darkened parts of the garage. But she had made it across alive. Now all she had to do was complete the return half of the journey.

There were no moving vehicles or people in sight: just the spare gauntlet of cars that flanked her route.

Once as she walked she looked back towards the office, which was of course illuminated, and saw the young guy bopping his head to the music from the Walkman he had on, and the sight reassured her. If he was not concerned, there was nothing to be concerned about.

Ralph actually seemed to be the jumpy one. As he went, he looked left and right at the cars that flanked them, but there was not much to see: The only light in the garage came from small caged overhead bulbs, and areas between and behind the cars were in darkness. It was not an ideal seeing situation for Emma anyway.

Her destination was an illuminated stairwell, and they were about halfway there when Ralph abruptly stopped, looking off towards the cars to the right. He growled.

"It's okay, baby," Emma said, "come on."

She pulled him forward. He was being spooked, she thought, by the sounds in there. A number of the cars, she thought, must have just been brought in, because their engines were making pinging sounds as they cooled, and twice she had heard an indeterminate gurgle.

But she also wondered why he would be spooked now, and not the first time they had passed this way.

Ten yards further on, there was another sound, a scraping sound, and Ralph stopped again, turned, and looked back. Ralph's normally benign facade was a mask of threat, his teeth bared, a low rumbling growl issuing from him.

Emma felt a chill.

She looked at the office again. The attendant was still listening to his music, business as usual.

"It's a roach or a mouse, bud. Come on."

Emma pulled Ralph forward again.

They had only gone a few yards when he stopped again, though there had been no sound, and looked at a very specific spot, the same spot he had looked at before: towards a bank of cars on her right, the fronts of which were dimly illuminated but the backs of which were in darkness.

But not total darkness. There were grades of darkness, Emma saw, and then she saw something that chilled her. The darkness seemed to move.

She blinked, striving to see. Could she trust her eyesight now? Was this a hallucination, poor eyesight, her own fear sort of projecting an image?

She could not tell for sure.

Suddenly, Ralph lurched forward, pulling the harness from her hand, and ran towards the spot in the darkness he had been watching.

"Ralph, no!"

Then he was swallowed up by the darkness.

Emma found herself walking towards the spot. She tried mightily to not make this more than it was.

"Ralph, come. Come!"

But there was nothing; not, weirdly, a sound. Maybe, she thought, Ralph was investigating. He became quiet when he investigated.

She whistled softly.

"Here, boy."

Now, she was being enveloped by the darkness herself, and it would have been hard enough for a fully sighted person to see. She couldn't, couldn't see Ralph . . . and then she spotted him, to the left, sniffing around an old car.

Emma came up to him. He seemed to have something in his mouth.

"If that's food," she said, "you're dead."

She leaned down and grasped his collar and pulled his head up.

There was something small and whitish hanging from his mouth.

It was a cross on a delicate chain. Byzantine. Silver.

"Silly," she said, taking the cross from his mouth.

She wondered what to do. Someone had probably dropped it. If she took it with her, they might return to look for it and not find it. She laid it back down on the concrete.

Then she started to stand up, and a movement in her right eye made her turn. She froze. There was a dark silhouette, a human form, standing between the fender and the wall.

She backed up a step, and turned, and screamed, her scream echoing in the garage, and started to run. She had no doubt that she was running for her life.

She was aware that the figure was behind her, intent to take her life, and then she heard Ralph, and glanced back, and he was running after the person pursuing her, barking insanely . . .

Then to her left, a flash of light and a car careened around the corner, its lights white and bright, and Emma was so glad to see it, and just got out of the way as it flashed by her, and she looked back and the figure was gone, but Ralph was directly in the beams, his eyes red and oh God there was a squeal of brakes but it was too late and Ralph was hit, and was knocked in the air, his body turning as if in slow motion, and then he came down with a terrible thump on the concrete.

"Ralph!"

Unaware of anything but Ralph, Emma ran over to him.

She cradled his head in her arms and started to cry. Behind her the driver had emerged from the car and approached.

"Ralph," she said softly, her voice—and her heart—breaking.

"I didn't see him," the driver said.

And the attendant, attracted by the commotion, was running towards them.

Emma was unaware. The only thing that mattered was Ralph.

25

· · ·

WHERE BEFORE THERE HAD BEEN ALMOST ABSO-lute darkness, now the garage level where Emma had been pursued was lit up by one-thousand-watt halogen lights as the cops made a detailed search for the man.

Leading the probe was Mitchell, but all the squad members were there.

Emma was in no shape to talk.

Ralph, still alive, was laid out on the desk in the guard booth. Standing near him was a cop. Dr. Pierce had materialized, and a veterinarian—lucki-ly at the hospital when the accident occurred—was examining Ralph.

Emma sat on the edge of the desk, tears in her eyes, constantly stroking Ralph.

John Hallstrom appeared. He set a cup of coffee on the desk next to Emma.

Unexpectedly, Ralph yelped in pain.

"Both legs are fractured," said the vet, a youngish-looking man who was prematurely bald. "Two broken ribs on the right. Tender spots, but no internal bleeding. He needs to go to the hospital."

"Let's go," Emma said.

Hallstrom's face screwed up. "You can't leave . . ."

"If we don't get to the hospital we're going to lose this dog," the vet said.

Mitchell came to the door of the booth. "Let her go. There's nothing out there."

Emma looked up.

"He was there," Emma said.

"Did you see him?" Mitchell asked.

"Not clearly . . ."

"Do you see anything clearly?"

"I smelled that same thing. That soap, that weird soap. I can still smell it now."

"What else?" Hallstrom asked.

"I found this cross or medallion. On the ground, and then I turned and he . . ."

Hallstrom shot Mitchell a sharp glance. "I never told her," he said.

Mitchell shook his head. "There's no cross."

Annoyed enough to leave Ralph, Emma left the booth and strode over to the place where she had first found the cross. It was not there.

Methodically, but quickly, she combed the ground to try to find it.

Nothing.

"It was here," she said. "I saw it . . . he must have picked it up."

Mitchell, who had followed, said to Hallstrom: "Car belongs to an old woman visiting her husband."

"Emma!" Pierce called from the booth.

Emma jogged back to the booth. Pierce and the vet were in the process of moving Ralph as gently and tenderly as possible to the back of the vet's station wagon.

They lay Ralph on a seat, and put a blanket on him. Emma sat down next to Ralph, Pierce helping her in as if she were a patient too.

Hallstrom watched.

"I want her," he said to Mitchell, "placed on twenty-four-hour protection. Paper the drawing all over the hospital."

"The drawing's a bust," Mitchell said.

"You saying she's lying?"

"I want to believe her," Mitchell said. "I want a witness as badly as you do. But I'm beginning to think this guy is a figment of her imagination."

"The guy was here."

"How do you know? It's not even in his pattern! He kills them in the home. You see a bathtub around here?"

"She's not part of his string, she's a witness. It's different. Maybe she doesn't fit his fucking psycho criteria. Maybe he was gonna take her somewhere, I don't know, but Mitch, she saw the cross."

"She could have overheard that in the precinct! The driver didn't see anyone, the guard here in the booth—there's no necklace."

Mitchell paused before continuing. "What," he said to Hallstrom, "do you know about this girl, John?"

"Just what I need to."

"Or what you want to. You haven't done your homework. She hallucinates, the doctor told me."

"We know that," Hallstrom said.

"Not the killer. She's seeing other things. From her past. It's not normal. Look, somebody was murdered in her building, she's afraid, her mind makes this stuff up."

"Something happened to her tonight," Hallstrom said flatly.

"The girl's a dead end. She hasn't led us anywhere. How many times are you gonna jump when she cries wolf?"

Hallstrom looked toward the station wagon.

Mitchell's comment had stung, perhaps because it was true. He did not know how many times he was going to jump. But it wasn't right now.

He watched Pierce lean down and kiss Emma on the cheek through the window. Vaguely, it bothered him. He watched the car as it slowly pulled away, then went out of sight.

Hallstrom turned back to Mitchell.

"She's all I got," Hallstrom said. "This guy's stumped me. You've always trusted my instincts."

"You stuffed your instinct in the trunk, John, and your dick's driving the car. Why don't you just fuck her and get on with the case?"

"I don't want to *fuck* her."

"What, you want to pick out china?"

"You're wrong."

"Okay. Show me. Assign her a uniform. And see how long you can stay away from her."

Hallstrom looked at him. Yes, he thought, he was wrong.

26
· · ·

Emma's apartment was in total darkness— which was just the way she wanted it.

The trip from the animal hospital where they had brought Ralph was painful, and not only because of her concern for Ralph. Certain realities had been encroaching on her, and for just this time she wanted to be alone and in the dark as she had so many times in her life. The dark held a special solace for her.

She was sitting on the couch in the living room, listening to the sounds of the night. The gurgle of pipes, the distant slam of a door, a honk.

But of course, no sound from the apartment above.

She tried to shut her mind down, shut out everything for just a little while.

Slowly, gratefully, she started to feel sleepy, to drift off . . .

Then she heard a sound, a soft, steady rap . . . and she opened her eyes.

Someone was knocking at the door. It would, she thought, be insane for the killer to just come here and knock on the door.

Slowly, she made her way to the door and, chain still on, opened the two locks and peered out.

It was John Hallstrom. Parked in a chair in the hall behind him was someone who she assumed was a cop, and in fact was Crowe, one of the cops that had been with Hallstrom the night he had done his striptease.

"Isn't," Emma said, "one of you enough?"

Hallstrom handed her a couple bars of soap. She sniffed them.

"That's not it."

"Is the dog all right?" Hallstrom asked.

"He has to stay there awhile."

Emma took the chain off and opened the door wide. Hallstrom, unbidden, came in. Crowe stayed outside.

Automatically, he ran a hand up and down the wall adjacent to the door frame looking for a light switch.

"Don't turn on the light," Emma said.

He stopped trying and she closed the door, plunging the apartment into total darkness.

He followed Emma, as best he could, into the living room. She went in as if equipped with radar. Hallstrom promptly had a minor collision with the couch.

"Do you want somethig to drink?" Emma asked.

Hallstrom had found the arm of the couch.

"I'm not staying," he said. He was disturbed by

her behavior. It seemed slightly bizarre.

Hallstrom heard her go into another room, then ice being dropped in a glass and her pouring something. She came back into the room and sat on the couch.

They sat in silence, except for the ice tinkling and the sound of Emma drinking. Then Hallstrom, who had found the shape of a lamp in the darkness, turned it on.

"What are you trying to do here?" he asked.

Emma covered her eyes with a throw pillow. "Turn that off, please."

"You think having the lights off is going to make everything okay?"

"Just let me pretend for a while."

"Pretend what? That you can't see?"

She pulled the pillow off her face with a violent motion. Words gushed out of her, words filled with anger and sadness and anxiety.

"I *can't* see! I can't see! Just like when I was little . . . only instead of blackness there's too much light. I can't see things that are right in front of me and I *can* see things that *couldn't be there*. For all I know it was Cuchetto in the hallway that night. I saw Valerie after she died. I saw my mother . . ." Emma stopped, almost choking on her words. "You want to see me cry? Boo-hoo, my dog got hit by a Buick. Now get the fuck out of here."

She reached over and turned off the lamp. Hallstrom turned it on again.

From his pocket, he produced two crosses and held them towards her. They were Celtic crosses inlaid with green jade.

"Is this the cross you saw?"

She shook her head no.

"You're always testing me," she said.

He took out another cross and held it up. This one froze Emma. It was the Byzantine cross.

She reached over and touched it. "That's the one."

"Why didn't you tell me about those other hallucinations?" he said softly.

" 'Cause it wouldn't make me a credible witness. Isn't that right? Isn't that what you're here to tell me? I'm a nut and you're moving on."

"No. Why do you think I've assigned someone to protect you?"

"I can protect myself."

"With what? Darkness? Just because you can't see what's out there doesn't mean it's gone."

"I survived twenty years without sight. Or a policeman at my door."

She turned the light off again—and Hallstrom turned it back on.

"Closing your eyes doesn't make you safe. It makes you stupid. Especially without the dog."

Startling him, Emma pushed the lamp off the table—and it crashed on the floor.

"You gonna break every lamp in the house?"

"No, but I'll take the bulbs out."

With that, she got up—and tripped over Hallstrom's foot, falling to the floor.

Hallstrom had noticed another lamp on a small table within reaching distance. He turned it on.

"Need some light?" he said.

"You fucking bastard."

Without warning, Emma grabbed his ankles and pulled hard. He lost his balance and fell to the floor. She was on him in an instant, a wild animal.

"Who," she half yelled, "do you think you are?"

"Hey, hey . . ."

Emma was determined to do him some bodily harm, and they thrashed around on the floor. Finally, some of her punches and kicks started to connect, and Hallstrom slammed her arms to the floor and pinned her with his body, his face close to hers.

"Lay down!" he said passionately. "Just lay down! Listen to me! Don't you cave in on me. You cave in, you die. Maybe there's only three people in the world who believe what you saw, but they're three dangerous motherfuckers. You, me, and the killer. If you want to keep your ass alive, you gotta help me. You gotta be strong."

Their eyes were locked. Emma's eyes narrowed.

"Strong. Like you?" she said.

"I've trained myself to look at it, what nobody else can look at. Calmly. Without emotion. So maybe I can help stop it."

She bucked—and he was thrown off. Quickly, she was on her feet.

"You're not strong," she spat.

"Don't test me."

She looked down at his fingers gripping her arm like a vise. "Your arms feel like they look."

He loosened his grip, and she turned her face up towards him. All he had to do was tilt his face down and they would kiss. But he didn't. He released her.

"Why did you come here?" Emma said.

"You, uh, need to get some sleep."

"I don't want to sleep."

Subtly, her body posture changed. Her chest went

out, her legs spread slightly, her face turned up. It was subtle—but clear.

Hallstrom got the message.

"I gotta go," Hallstrom said almost sheepishly.

He turned and walked to the door. Her words caught him, stopped him just before he passed outside.

"Someday," she said, "that dam you built's gonna break, Hallstrom. It's only bones and skin. And it's gonna hurt when the water blasts through."

The door shut behind him.

27

• • •

LATE IN THE AFTERNOON TWO DAYS AFTER HE HAD left Emma's apartment—in fact it was St. Patrick's Day—John Hallstrom was in his office. Arrayed on his desk were many of the photographs related to the case, and other evidence, including the crosses that had been found at the crime scenes.

But Hallstrom had come across something else that interested him even more: The *Sun-Times* article on Emma Brody.

As he read it, he could imagine the kind of chaos her life must have been. To be a little girl, to lose your sight after having known it and to be deserted by your mother. Blind, alone, unloved. A heavy fucking burden.

Shit like this, he thought, was even worse than homicide. He had known quite a few cops who had worked Family Court—which handled cases like Emma's—but few worked it for long without the help of alcohol. It shredded the soul, and you had to get out before that happened.

His mind shifted away as Ridgely came into the room. Hallstrom had wanted to show him something.

Hallstrom waved a hand, beckoning him to look at a lineup of dispensers of liquid soap on the desk. Ridgely looked carefully.

"Where'd you get these?" he asked.

"The hospital. Anti-bacterial. Surgical, etcetera, etcetera. She saw him there last night, she smelled the weird soap."

"So you're bringing her in for a detergical lineup, like some kinda goddamn commercial?"

"What are *you* doing? Anyone at the Byzantine churches recognize the drawing?"

The PA interrupted Ridgely's response. "Hallstrom, line 501!"

He picked it up. It was Crowe.

Ridgely saw the color drain from Hallstrom's face.

"Yeah, what? You *lost* her?" he said. Then, he hung up and was gone from the office.

A HALF HOUR later, after a Mario-Andretti–type ride, Hallstrom was standing in the midst of a bunch of drunks who were doing their best to celebrate St. Patrick's Day. Behind them, marchers went by.

Crowe was totally embarrassed. "She wanted to see the floats," he said.

" . . . asshole rookie fuckup . . ."

"Then this lady asked me to take the picture."

" . . . jerk mother jag-off . . ."

"I should have known when she wanted to bring the violin."

"She had the violin?"

HALLSTROM GOT BACK in the car.

The violin, he thought, the violin.

His mind went back to the article in the *Sun-Times*.

Her name, the agent's name, was Candice Archer. If anyone had a shot at knowing where Emma was, it was her.

Then, a montage of images hit him, like a fast slide show. Of two bodies, strangled, wrists slit neatly . . . of Emma . . .

Yes, he had to find Candice Archer. He had to find Emma.

28

· · ·

THE ALGONBLICK PUB, WHICH WAS NOT TOO FAR from O'Flaherty's, was a long way from it in other ways.

For one thing, it appealed to a different kind of clientele. At O'Flaherty's the setting was almost raucous. It was a fairly large place where people came to drink, play, and dance hard to foot-stomping Irish folk music.

The Algonblick was much more intimate, a small room which held fewer than a hundred people. The lighting was muted, the conversation soft, the people much older and more cerebral and into the music being offered.

And the offerings were quite different. On any given night at the Algonblick you could hear a grade-six violinist—they resented the term fiddler and there were no beginners at the Algonblick— playing pieces penned by Mozart and Tchaikovsky, or movie music, or experimental compositions that appealed to a handful of people, and sometimes to no one except the people who had created them. Or you could hear a skilled quartet or trio play traditional Irish folk songs.

On any given night Emma could have fit in well at the Algonblick, and that's where she was now—herself on the violin, Michael playing the guitar, and Winston singing.

The crowd, mostly of Irish heritage, was collectively entranced by the sweet sounds coming from the trio.

And so were Sean and Candice Archer, sitting in the audience.

And Emma was back, musically speaking.

Her bow hand stroked the strings, occasionally hitting a harmonic—the highest sound a violin can hit—the sound piercing, and piercingly beautiful.

Emma's eyes were closed and she was totally inside the music—and outside looking in wonderingly, her head occasionally tilting forward, then back, throwing her lovely hair, making it glisten in the single spotlight.

Across the room John Hallstrom stood against a wall and watched her.

The music and the sight of her were doing things to his stomach. She was beautiful, gorgeous, but there was a sensitivity about her—as most definitely evinced by her music. He wanted to stop looking at her, wanted to try to retreat back to get some distance on her, but he could not. His eyes were riveted on her.

Then the trio finished the piece with a long harmonic. She opened her eyes and smiled.

There was polite applause—it almost seemed in bad taste to stand up and cheer, though the audience was by no means pretentious—and that was that.

Later, Emma busied herself putting her violin in its case.

Something to the side of her caught her attention and she looked up—into the face of John Hallstrom.

In his eyes she saw a softness she had never seen before . . . something beautiful which she couldn't quite define.

Neither said a word for a moment, and then Hallstrom did:

"Ready to go?"

A voice cut in from his left and Hallstrom turned, momentarily not recognizing who it was. He was accustomed to seeing him in whites. It was Dr. Ryan Pierce, dressed in designer jeans and a tweed jacket.

Normally he wore glasses, but now he had contacts on. It gave a better symmetry to his face. He seemed much better-looking.

"Um, Dr. Pierce, you know the detective . . ."

"Yes. What are you doing here?" said Pierce.

Somehow, Hallstrom felt a surge of anger. "I'm doin' my fuckin' job, pal. What are *you* doin' here?"

Pierce did not answer.

Then Sean and Candice joined the group.

"Sounded good, Emma," Candice said.

Emma looked at Candice, and Emma's look said everything. "Candice . . ."

"You don't have to say anything."

"Yes, I do."

114

They joined hands. Then Candice glanced at first Pierce and then Hallstrom, who was still feeling bilious.

"Which one's your date, Grumpy or Doc?"

"Where are your glasses?" Hallstrom asked Pierce.

"Contacts, I'm wearing . . ." he answered. "Are you . . . does he . . . have to come with us?"

Emma's silence was her answer.

A HALF HOUR later, Pierce and Emma were settled in at a table in the middle of the room of an elegant restaurant. John Hallstrom, like some bird of prey, was standing at a balcony bar looking down at them.

Throughout the meal, Emma and Pierce seemed to enjoy each other's company. Hallstrom watched them in stony silence.

A half hour later they left the restaurant. Hallstrom continued to watch them, this time from his car as he inched along State Street and they walked along, arm in arm, until they reached Pierce's Mercedes.

As far as he was able to see, there was no killer skulking around. But in his business you could never be sure. He didn't want to get himself—as well as Emma and her newfound boyfriend—into a situation without backup.

He was glad when they got into the car.

As they drove, Hallstrom kept on their tail, observing their body language as they went, but there was nothing unusual. Both looked straight ahead.

Hallstrom was aware that he should keep his mind on his job.

29

• • •

Pierce drove Emma home, and they started up the steps to her building. The street was empty, apparently, except for them—and Hallstrom, who had parked across the street some fifty yards down and was walking up it in the direction of Emma's building. He watched them intently.

Pierce nodded slightly, then placed his hands on Emma's shoulders and kissed her . . . kissed her like someone who was in love with her would kiss her.

Then his eyes clouded over . . . and he walked away. The signs were subtle, but definite: It would not work.

Emma watched him go, and then she turned and looked across the street.

Hallstrom stood there, looking at her.

In the next few moments, no words were spoken, no gestures made, but Hallstrom started walking across the street, and climbed the steps to the stoop.

And no words were exchanged either when they both silently entered her building.

After all, he did have to protect her, didn't he?

THE CHAIR THAT Crowe had used when he parked himself outside Emma's apartment was still in the hall, but neither Emma nor Hallstrom gave more than a moment's consideration to whether Hallstrom would use it and stay outside.

He followed her into the apartment, and a few minutes later watched as, silently, she went over to a window that fronted the street and looked out. She was bathed in moonlight. He stood like a statue, his hands in his pockets.

He did not want to say anything warm or intimate, but he did.

"I read that story . . . about you."

It wasn't just the words, but the way he said them. Soft, concerned, a far cry from Hallstrom the cop.

She said nothing.

Again, something surged from him. It was as if he were listening to things someone else was uttering. But he had to say it anyway.

"So, you and the doctor . . ."

"I wanted to get on with my life. But I just can't see him that way."

"See?"

She turned from the window and walked slowly toward him, so beautiful and seductive as to be almost an apparition.

"My eyes are all filled with someone else."

Hallstrom looked at her. His belly was tight. For really the first time he noticed the color of her eyes . . . dark brown. It was hard to believe that just a short while ago they were glazed and white.

She reached up and touched his cheek . . .

As if magnetized, unable to violate a natural attraction, like a planet turning on its axis, he slowly turned his head so his lips touched her fingers . . .

"Let me see you with my hands . . ." Emma said.

Her hands moved down to his chest.

" . . . with my body . . . with my tongue."

She pressed into him, and he felt the soft voluptuousness of her body against his. He tried to fight it, tried not to do this—Mitchell was right—but then he felt himself straining inside, and his mouth found her, and then their tongues were exploring and something deep inside him moved, and he felt the dam release, gushing, gushing, gushing . . . and it was not painful, but good . . . oh, so very good.

30

. . .

Hallstrom woke up late the next morning, a rarity for him. Normally, he would be up by five, whether he had a tour that day or not. It was just part of the pell-mell pace he constantly traveled at.

Today he woke up at seven—mid-afternoon—took a leisurely shower, and used one of Emma's razors to shave.

As he dressed in her bedroom, he looked at her.

He was, he knew, attractive to women, and hardly a day had gone by when he awoke alone in his room—unless he'd wanted to be alone.

But that was a different kind of being with someone. He would wake up with a body by his side, sometimes a body he didn't recognize.

But this beautiful woman was more than a body. Much more. He knew that, and it scared him. It had been years—and years—since he had been involved seriously with any woman. Why? He didn't spend a lot of time analyzing. There was Gina, the one great love of his life, whom he had loved when a teenager, but that hadn't worked out. Since then he had never gotten that involved with any woman. In fact, the sexual conquests had somehow become part of the dam, as Emma called it. And Hallstrom was loath to explain it.

Finished dressing, Hallstrom took a long last look at her and felt his lips. They were a little puffy. He smiled. Small wonder. He had sucked many parts of her for a long time and that, he thought, was the wages of . . . whatever it was.

He started toward the front door. He wanted to check to see if Crowe had shown up. He'd been scheduled to come in at midnight the night before. Hallstrom had wanted to make sure that even if Emma were not found, no one could break into her apartment and give her an unpleasant surprise.

Now, if Crowe was there, Hallstrom had to have an excuse ready. And if not, he would call him and tell him to get his butt over here.

Hallstrom opened the door.

Crowe was there.

Hallstrom went on the attack, preempting a question. "You are in trouble. You would need flippers to wade through the shit you are in."

Crowe said nothing.

"The lady was so upset I had to sack out on her couch!"

Crowe continued to stare at him. There was more watchfulness than fear in his eyes.

"I'm gonna have to write this up."

Crowe remained mute.

120

"But I'll tell you want. Here's what we're gonna do. 'Cause I like you. I won't report this little incident, if you keep quiet about me sleeping on the lady's couch. Deal?"

Crowe spoke. For the first time, Crowe spoke. "Deal, sir," he said.

LATER THAT MORNING, Emma awakened, the memory of the night before thrumming through her body and mind.

Hallstrom, she saw, had left, but that didn't matter. In a very real sense he was still with her, and she knew that he was going to be with her a long time.

Last night had been a revelation. The dam inside Hallstrom had indeed burst—and so had a dam inside herself. She had not only been able to feel him with all her finely tuned senses, but *see* him. Actually see him, in fine detail, up close, and in living color.

He was delicious.

And of course her heart had seen him also, and what it had seen she loved very much. He was tender, caring, loving—just what she had always known.

She got out of bed and went over to the closet door to get her robe—and was surprised, and pleased: Hallstrom had taken the blanket away.

She looked at herself in the mirror. Not bad, she chuckled, not bad.

She stretched, yawned, strolled into the living room.

Bars of sunlight streamed in the window and highlighted—a surprise.

In the center of the coffee table was a gorgeous bouquet of roses, a brilliant burst of red. There was a big card propped against it. It said, in large letters, "SPECIAL DELIVERY . . . FROM TIR NA NOG."

Emma picked up the card and her vision clouded, this time not from a physical impairment, but from something else—tears . . . of joy.

31

. . .

THE HOUSE LOOKED LIKE ANY OTHER ON ANY OTH-
er upper-middle–class suburban street in America.
It was a colonial-style, painted white with powder-
blue trim, and in the back was a cedar deck which
the owners had recently finished with a clear water-
proofer that would also preserve the wood and protect it from graying. The house, like others in the
development, was set on a half acre of flat, meticulously coiffed lawn.

But it was not a museum. Secured to the front of
the house was a battered hoop and backboard. They
had gotten a lot of use.

The lady of the house, in her thirties, was typical
also of suburban women. She was fighting a battle,
this one against the bulge. And it had been a long
one, and she had utilized various cures including
Nutra System, Weight Watchers, Jenny Craig, Diet
Center, Topps, and Optifast.

The battle had gone on for about five years, after the birth of her third child, Lea, and more than once she had thought she could never win it. Food was the way she dealt with anxiety. Have a little free-floating anxiety? Scarf a half-dozen Dunkin Donuts and it would go away. A little anxiety about the extra gray hair? Gobble some—or a lot of—Taco Bell. Have a vague suspicion that your hubby, Ray, was seeing another woman—slim, of course, with muscle tone and tits like cantaloupes? Buy a box of chocolate donuts and keep them in the laundry hamper for easy access.

Now, though, she had been winning the war with the use of diet pills and drugs, though there were some undesirable side effects. And, of course, there were occasional setbacks. And that was what she was talking about now with her friend Marlene on a cordless phone.

She was in the kitchen as she spoke. "And my face is so fat, I think Ray doesn't want to sleep with me anymore."

She listened as her friend spoke, then responded, at the same time suffering a little setback—she unloaded the makings of a sandwich from the refrigerator.

"It's the medication," she said. Then, after listening: "No, they're not here. Ray took them to the movies."

As her friend spoke, the woman looked around the kitchen, contemplating the deliciousness of it. It had only recently been remodeled, and in it were $15,000 worth of new custom cabinets, a new post-form countertop, all-new appliances, and a ceramic-tile floor that could resist dynamite and the more usual assaults from the kids.

"Come over," she said. "Aw, come on. I haven't felt this good in years."

And she was preoccupied. So much so that she didn't notice the slight shift of light in the room, as if caused by someone or something passing across the task lights under the countertop.

"Okay, okay . . . yes . . . okay . . . honestly, Marlene, I'm not made of glass . . . bye."

She turned the phone off with a sigh, set it on the countertop, and started to salivate.

Then she could not breathe. A tremendous force was being exerted on her neck, and she tried to scream, but all she was aware of was that her eyes were popping, bursting almost, and as heavy as she was, she felt herself being lifted from the floor.

Gradually, she realized she was losing consciousness, and she cried for her babies and then her mother and something broke in her neck, and then the blackness oozed in around her.

A minute later, she was dead and she was dropped on the floor like a sack of vegetables.

The perp looked at her. In one hand was a Byzantine cross. In the other was a scalpel.

Now, he thought, the necessary work would be completed.

32
* * *

SOME MAJOR LEAGUE BALLPARKS WERE HAPPILY
situated for people who didn't mind a long-range
view of the game—for unbeatable prices. Such folks
simply broke out their deck chairs, loaded up with a
plentiful supply of snacks and drinks and whatever
else made things comfortable, and climbed to the
roof. Some could even see games from their windows.
With the help of a radio, to fill in whatever couldn't
be seen, everything worked out well.

Wrigley Field was one such ballpark. From rooftops on Sheffield Avenue, including the roof on the
apartment house where John Hallstrom lived, one
had a tremendous view of the game, and that was
where Emma and John Hallstrom were now.

Emma and Hallstrom were not alone. Indeed,
there were a half-dozen other folks—including a
few non-residents who had paid the super for these
"tar beach" spots—and they were there to view the

Cubs' first night game of the season.

At just about game time, Hallstrom and Emma were standing at the parapet of the building, looking down and across into the brightly lit field. Hallstrom watched her. Wind touseled her hair a bit, and his view had a similar effect on his insides.

Hallstrom handed her a pair of binoculars. She looked through them, then put the glasses down and turned to Hallstrom.

"I have no idea what I'm looking at. It's either a base pad or Sandberg's butt."

From the back, an old man yelled: "Down in front."

Hallstrom turned and smiled. "Emma," he said, "this is Rex."

Rex responded with a grunt, and then Hallstrom began introducing her to everyone else.

"Sue and Bridget . . . Matt 'The Stat' Mossbacher, Dave, Kenneth, Mr. and Mrs. Goldman . . ."

The Goldmans, an older couple, nodded and smiled and said, "The Goldmans," their assumption being that something was wrong with Emma's hearing. Then Mrs. Goldman added: "First night game of the season. They're having fireworks."

A few minutes later the fireworks began, and it was exciting and beautiful, a kaleidoscope of colors exploding with loud pops over the stadium, all the faces of the fans turned upward.

But Hallstrom hardly noticed. He could not stop looking at Emma. She stroked his back. She saw a certain expression in his face, a silence, a brooding silence.

Suddenly the sky exploded in a frenzy of color and sound, the grand finale, and when it ended the fans roared and clapped appreciatively. Then, there was just smoke drifting across the sky.

THROUGH MOST OF the game, Hallstrom was silent, but he was saying something with his glances, his body language.

Then someone smacked a home run, and the ball soared onto Sheffield Avenue, where a bunch of kids scrambled after it.

Hallstrom smiled. He remembered something.

"When I was about ten, I was working the street with my mitt and my friend Andy, and Hank Aaron hit a home run right into my glove. And I wanted to keep it, God, did I want it. And everybody's shouting, 'Throw it back,' and I took off running. Burst into that building, over there, up to the roof, and three big assholes with 'Cubs' tattooed on their knuckles chased me across the rooftops, all along there, like the Chimney Sweeps in *Mary Poppins*."

His voice trailed off. Emma smiled. She realized that what he was saying to her had nothing to do with baseball, and everything to do with letting her inside him, the place where his heart hid.

Hallstrom looked at her. "What?"

She said nothing. She let her soft smile do the talking.

"Let's go in," he said.

IN HIS BEDROOM, Emma and Hallstrom stood facing each other. A nearby lamp provided the only illumination, and Emma reached to turn it off. Hallstrom stopped her.

Slowly he began to unbutton her blouse, and then she helped, and he undressed her and himself and

128

they were both nude, and he picked her up and she wrapped her legs around his waist and he slowly entered her, filling her up, and her eyes closed . . .

"Open your eyes," he said.

She did. He started to move back and forth in her, his strong arms holding her with ease, and she reached down and clutched his round, muscular butt and pulled him into herself as deep as he could go . . .

"I want you to look at me," he said. "Look at me . . ."

She did, and if Hallstrom thought of something else to say he could not say it. He could hardly breathe. The pleasure was intense, and then got even better and they went into a rhythm, each stroke unbearably delicious, and the best part was that their eyes were open, glazed, yet on fire . . . and then Emma started to shudder, gasp, and Hallstrom did too, and they figuratively and literally started to empty themselves in each other . . . their bodies one, not knowing where one began and one left off, and then, unexpectedly, but not caring, Hallstrom was thrown off balance, and they gently toppled onto the bed and continued to shudder until finally they stopped, and they lay there side by side, empty, light as feathers, yet filled to the brim.

THE NEXT MORNING, Emma sat at a table in one of Hallstrom's large T-shirts, picking out and eating ligonberries—they looked like small blueberries but were not as sweet—from a bowl on the counter. Hallstrom was at the nearby stove, naked except for shorts, cooking a small mountain of flapjacks.

Emma eyed him as he worked.

Then the El train went by with about a 3.2 on the Richter scale, rattling the dishes—and the house—and Emma interrupted his thoughts.

"Do you ever get used to that?" Emma asked.

"Used to what?" he answered, not knowing what her question meant.

Emma smiled, then wandered out of the kitchen. She was anxious to just know him.

In one room, there was a bookcase full of books. Hallstrom had come in behind her.

"What are these, textbooks?" she asked.

"Don't look at those."

She tried to read one, but her eyes were not quite up to the task.

"What's this one say?"

"Uh . . . nineteenth-century poetry."

"You taking classes?"

He did not answer.

Then she picked up a picture showing Hallstrom escorting a dangerous-looking person.

"Who's in this picture?"

"You don't want to know," Hallstrom said. "Breakfast is almost ready."

"Am I making you nervous?"

"No."

"I think I am."

Hallstrom smiled. "I'm tryin' to think if I locked up my gun."

She held up some CD's for him to read.

"Van Morrison, Vivaldi, and the Tijuana Brass . . ."

"Eclectic," Emma said.

"The Drovers . . ."

"You're kidding. When did you . . ."

"That night I saw you guys they were selling 'em in the lobby."

"You're one of the three people who bought one."

"I'm all three people," he said, and Emma smiled. "Irish, we gotta stick together. I figured I could give 'em as Christmas presents."

Emma followed Hallstrom back into the kitchen. She leaned on the counter and looked at him as he went back to complete the cooking.

"I think I could fall in love with you."

Hallstrom was silent.

"Did you hear what I said?"

Hallstrom was in the process of placing ligonberries on top of the steaming pancakes, then rolling them up.

"I heard you," he said. "Thank you."

"You're welcome."

He handed her her plate.

"I gotta go to work today," he said.

Emma looked at him and nodded. "Right," she said flatly. It was almost, she thought, funny.

Abruptly, the wall phone rang.

Hallstrom picked up. "Hallstrom . . . what . . . yes. Yes. I'll be right there."

He hung up, ashen. "There's been another murder. In Milwaukee."

33

· · ·

Hallstrom got to the El station as quickly as he could, bringing Emma with him. The trip was made in silence, Hallstrom apparently preoccupied with the new killing. When he arrived at the precinct he asked Emma to wait on a bench in the hall. Then he went with Ridgely, who had spotted Emma, into the interior offices.

"What's she doing here?" Ridgely asked.

Hallstrom responded with a question of his own. "How long was this one dead when they found her?"

"Not even an hour. The husband came home with the kids."

Hallstrom felt anger building as he approached and then went into his office. The lineup of soap dispensers was still there, mute testimony to his efforts so far.

Abruptly, savagely, he swept them off with his hand.

Ridgely looked through Hallstrom's door, then through the hall door. The angle was such that it enabled him to see Emma.

"Are you in trouble, John?"

Hallstrom was mute. Ridgely tried again. "What's going on with this girl?"

"None of your business," Hallstrom shot back.

"It is my business!" Ridgely retorted. "It's my ass here. Mitchell's talking about putting another team on."

"What? Mitchell is what? Where did you hear that? What are we not doing? We have followed every lead and every one is a blind fuckin' alley but her. She keeps knockin' like a kid on Halloween. She's the key, Tommy, I'm telling you."

"To the case or to you?"

Hallstrom could have fought back, but suddenly he was tired by it all. He sat down and sank into his chair. "I brought her flowers, Ridge. Me. I bought her fuckin' flowers."

Mitchell loomed in the doorway. "There you are," he said.

"What have we got?" Hallstrom asked.

"She's a plump, yuppie mom."

"Great," Hallstrom said, "A petite little co-ed, a five-eleven blond grocery checker . . ."

"Somebody's got to call Milwaukee and tell them we've got jack-shit and it's not going to be me." Mitchell paused, then continued looking directly at Hallstrom. "Be sure to show them the drawing you got from a blind witness."

"You keep pushing me."

"You need it!"

"Then take me off the case."

"No fuckin' way. You are goin' right down with me, asshole. I got two city chiefs riding my back and you know more about this case than anyone. This guy's beating you, man. This guy's out there laughing at you. You go after him. You better shut him down, 'cause you're not getting off this case. You're gonna retire on this one."

Later, Hallstrom came out of the office, into the hall. He paused and looked down at Emma, still on the bench.

"I'm going to Milwaukee. Don't ask me when I'll be back because I don't know."

WHEN EMMA GOT home, her emotions were still in a jumble over her encounter with Hallstrom in the hall. The ice had gone around him again, and she felt like a Ping-Pong ball. A very used one.

She very much wanted to write him off, to block him out of her mind, but in her heart she knew she couldn't.

She took her coat off, then proceeded to the bedroom closet and opened the door to hang up the garment.

Suddenly she was immobile with fear. Staring out at her from the mirror on the back of the door were two blood-red eyes, drawn in lipstick.

She blinked and blinked and blinked . . . but the eyes did not go away.

34

• • •

Now the house of the "plump yuppie," as she had been rather callously described by Mitchell, had been transformed from a cookie-cutter suburban home to a place where ghouls gathered. It was night, so it seemed particularly appropriate.

Across the street, neighbors and neighbors' kids clustered, but there were also people from other areas—and some who masqueraded as people—who had heard about the killing in the media and made sure they were there.

And, of course, there might be a killer there—particularly, as the FBI and experienced cops like Hallstrom would say, a killer who was involved in what amounted to multiple fetishistic murder. The post-homicidal habits of such killers often included a visit to the murder scene. A little after-dinner drink.

Which was why, just down the block, there was

parked a battered van half primed and half finish-painted, on the inside of which were two FBI agents, one taking photos of the crowd and jotting down the plate number of every car that came down the block and parked or kept going, and the other videotaping everything. If there was someone on that block who didn't have an explanation for being there, the FBI and the local gendarmes would, as the cop saying goes, "look up his ass with a microscope."

John Hallstrom's would be one of the plate numbers taken, because around nine P.M. he pulled up in front of the block in a rental car and started to walk up the driveway to the house.

As he walked, he noticed that, oddly, a boy of maybe eleven or twelve was shooting baskets into a hoop on the front of the house. It seemed odd, considering what had happened in the house.

Hallstrom stopped. "Shouldn't you be at home getting ready for bed, kid?"

The kid sunk one, but did not answer.

Hallstrom stood watching the kid play for a minute. He sensed the kid wanted to say something.

He was right.

"You here for the murder? They're all inside."

"You live here?"

The kid nodded. Hallstrom could tell he was holding back tears.

"I'm sorry," Hallstrom said.

The kid stopped, swallowed hard. "Why do people say that? Why don't they say it sucks shit! Your mom's dead!"

"Kid, it sucks shit. Your mom's dead."

The kid dribbled back to the net. Hallstrom turned and looked at him once more before passing inside.

136

• • •

INSIDE THE HOUSE, Hallstrom met David Frank, a tough-looking Milwaukee cop. They stood in a hall and Hallstrom filled him in on their non-existent progress in Chicago.

"We'll be coming to Chicago tomorrow," Frank said.

"I wish I had more for you."

"Sometimes it takes a new victim, new input to the case to break it open."

"Tell that to *them*," Hallstrom said, leaning his head towards a doorway which lead to the kitchen. Inside was an older lady who was obviously one of the grandmas. She had a little girl sitting in her lap. There was a priest off to one side, talking to someone from the ME's office.

Hallstrom could hear the priest talking, and he listened.

"But she marked her driver's license," the priest said. "It was important for her to donate her . . . you can imagine . . ."

"The autopsy makes it impossible," the ME guy said. "I'm sorry, Father, but even if we could, she lost too much blood from the wrist wounds for them to be in any shape. . . ."

Hallstrom walked down the hallway, and glanced into the living room. There was something on the carpet . . . flowers. It looked like a bouquet of roses, wrapped in green paper, but they were browning, dead.

Hallstrom went in and touched the flowers. Then he heard a voice from behind him.

"I brought those home. Last night. For her."

Hallstrom turned. It was, he assumed, the victim's

husband. He was an ordinary-looking guy dressed in a white shirt, tie, gray pants. Hallstrom imagined him as a stockbroker, something white collar.

Hallstrom kept quiet, not knowing quite what to say.

The husband did. "How many has he killed?"

"As far as we know . . . three."

"Including my wife?"

"Your wife is number three."

"Don't call her a number. Don't give her a number."

The husband crossed the room and picked up a color family picture, one that had obviously been done by a professional photographer, everyone smiling and looking their best for just this moment.

Hallstrom looked. He recognized the kid who was playing basketball, but he was five years younger. The woman was dark-haired, pretty, and at least in the picture didn't seem that plump.

"Her name's Margaret Tatterstall," said the husband.

"I'm sorry, sir."

The husband looked at Hallstrom. His eyes teared and he spoke in a low, soft tone. In fact, he was having difficulty speaking.

"What have you been doing down there? Why didn't you catch him?"

Hallstrom was at a loss to answer.

"What," the man repeated, his voice suffused with sadness and anger, "have you been doing?"

Hallstrom just looked at him.

HALLSTROM SPENT ABOUT an hour at the house, talking with the lead detective, some FBI guys, and the ME. The woman had been strangled, her wrists slashed—and that silver Byzantine cross placed on her. But as far as he could tell, they had nothing, no leads. The FBI would profile the scene, and that might yield something, but only time would tell.

There were still ghouls across the street when he got into the rental car, but before he could turn the key he was suffused with his own sense of sadness.

Yes, he had told Emma, he had trained himself to look at things other people could not look at.

But for some reason, he was having trouble looking at this. Real trouble.

The kid was no longer playing basketball.

And the kid, he thought, would no longer be called in by his mother for dinner.

His eyes misted. No, he was not looking at this one too well at all. And he didn't like the feeling. He felt himself pulling inside, making an effort to pull himself out of it. Homicide, he thought, had no room for tears. And if you did cry, there were things you could miss, and a killer would kill again.

He started the car and drove into the night.

35

. . .

It took Hallstrom almost four hours to drive from Milwaukee to his apartment. It wasn't traffic that got in the way. It was himself. He just did not feel like getting back to Chicago rapidly.

On the way, he thought about what he had seen in Milwaukee, and he nursed a lingering doubt about his role in the death of Margaret Tatterstall. Maybe if he hadn't been involved with Emma, the woman would still be alive.

He knew, deep down, that it was an outlandish idea, that at root it was not terribly logical, that he was not responsible for anything.

Yes, fine, tell that to his stomach.

Despite trying not to, he thought about Emma for a good portion of the trip.

Making love to her had been fantastic, and at one point he'd thought he might have a coronary. She was a wonderful lover, and so beautiful that even when he was right in the act, part of himself would look over his shoulder and a voice would tell him that this wasn't happening. But it surely had.

And he knew too that he could not see her again . . . at the same time realizing that that was going to be difficult . . . very difficult. Over the past few weeks she had shown up in the oddest places . . . in the clouds, the buildings, everywhere. Emma Brody had seeped into every aspect of his life.

It did scare him to get involved with her, and part of the reason—if he were brutally honest with himself—was that he had not been shown good things about love in his own house. His parents had fought constantly, and when they had divorced he was only six years old. Not exactly a blueprint for the bliss of married life or commitment.

But there was another, more pressing reason. He had to have a clear mind, to stand outside this thing as much as possible so he could protect her—and bring this fuck to earth. He couldn't do that while he was walking around in a haze.

But yes, it was going to be hard.

WHEN HE ENTERED his apartment, Hallstrom took a lesson from Emma. He left the lights off.

He went into the living room and just stood there in the darkness. He was tired. Deep tired in the body, and the soul.

In his bedroom, the phone rang—and he hoped to God this fuck hadn't done anyone else. He just didn't want to face that tonight.

He let his answering machine pick it up.

"Hallstrom. Leave a message."

"John, it's Emma. Are you back?"

Hallstrom stood like a tree rooted to the spot. What should he do? What? Then the decision was made for him. Emma hung up.

Then Hallstrom went into the bedroom and lay across the bed. He thought he would have trouble sleeping. He was wrong. Within minutes he was in a deep sleep.

36

* * *

IT WAS NIGHT. EMMA SAT ON A BENCH IN THE MIDDLE of the deserted El station platform on Addison Street, which was the closest stop to the precinct, and waited for the train to come in.

Her mind was troubled with thoughts of John Hallstrom; in fact, her mind was flooded with thoughts of John Hallstrom. But she knew that she had to put him to one side if she wanted to survive.

Putting things to one side was how she had survived her childhood, the days and nights with her mother and the foster homes and the cruelty of some kids because she was blind.

Somewhere, back there when she was a little girl, she'd decided that she would never give up. Fuck her mother, fuck Hallstrom, and fuck the world.

She would survive. She had before, and she would again.

But the knowledge of that did not help ease the pain now. It went deep, as deep as anything in her life. She loved John Hallstrom. It would be easier to say she was going to put him aside than to do it.

He was, she knew, trying to help her—in his own way. He was also trying to avoid involvement. Yes, he had his demons too.

She blinked, looked up and down the platform.

Empty.

What was she doing there? She could be in jeopardy. Someone had followed her, stalked her, broken into her apartment and drawn eyes on her mirror. Maybe Hallstrom had a point. She had to try thinking with her brain, not her heart.

Defiant, that's the way she had been her whole life. It had made her challenge her mother, and challenge the kids who harassed her, and she had never taken much shit from anyone.

But it could hurt her. Like now. She shouldn't be here.

Definitely.

She glanced to her right and gasped.

Someone was under the lamp but moving—towards her. A man. Though she could see well enough, she could not make out his features.

But his face seemd slightly angled so he was looking at her, not anywhere else.

She turned away. It was not the time to start building scary scenarios.

She listened for the train—willing it to come—but heard nothing.

A few seconds later she glanced back towards where the man was and blinked. He was getting closer. She didn't like it. She wanted the train to come, hoped it would come.

Please.

First she heard the tracks click, then in the distance the sound of the train: It was coming.

So, still, was the man. Emma got up and started walking down the platform, away from him.

As she walked, she glanced back over her shoulder. He was getting closer, and so was the train, but there was only so much platform.

It seemed endless, but it was only fifteen seconds or so before the train hammered into the station, and then its brakes went on in a cacophony that sounded like thousands of knives and forks being dumped on the tracks, and in that moment Emma turned to see if the man were still there, and he was . . . and he was the murderer.

She screamed, her scream reverberating in the train-braking sound, but then the train had stopped, the doors slid open, and she got on. And the murderer slipped on a couple of cars away.

Her car was empty. The doors closed, the train lurched and started.

She watched the windowed door at the end of her car. She thought about going to the conductor, but she didn't know where he was.

There was only one thing she could do.

Quickly she exited the car through an end door, and as she did her sight failed her just a bit and she had to take great care to insure that she did not fall between the cars.

She closed the door to the next car behind her, shutting out the deafening roar in the process, and looked into the car.

Relief flooded her. Down at the end, sitting together, were two women. She ran towards them, and just before she got to them they turned.

Her heart stopped. It was Valerie Wheaton. And there was another woman sitting next to her—it *had* to be Nina Getz.

She glanced behind, and through the glass saw the killer approaching the door.

She wanted to cry, but she had to fight.

How?

She ran out of the car, through to the next one, and there was someone else there . . . two women sitting at opposite sides of the car.

One woman turned towards her.

It was her mother, her wrinkled face framed by bleach-blond hair, smiling, showing yellow teeth and a red mouth, her teeth and her arms outstretched.

Behind her, she heard the door to the car slide open violently. She turned. He was inside the car, coming towards her, and she screamed, her screaming melding with the violent sound of the train, and she knew was going to die but she would fight to the end . . .

Then, he was upon her and . . . and she heard a familiar voice and a hand was on her shoulder rather than her neck . . .

"Ms. Brody, Ms. Brody. It's me. It's Ridgely. It's okay."

Emma looked, fully expecting to see the killer's face.

But it *was* Ridgely.

Unless it wasn't. Unless it was the killer who looked like Ridgely.

She looked at the spot where her mother was sitting and it was empty, and the woman on the other side approached her. It was a heavyset black woman—the train conductor.

"You all right, honey?" she asked, her face full of concern.

Emma looked at Ridgely. He was pissed.

"It's okay. You're okay. Don't you ever try to sneak off again, all right?"

Tears filled Emma's eyes. She put her hand over her eyes, eyes that had failed and tortured her.

37

. . .

JOHN HALLSTROM WAS ON THE JOB IN THE PRE-
cinct by seven in the morning, poring over the
evidence on the case trying to find . . . anything.

The FBI had called him from Quantico, Virginia,
where the agency had its famed Behavioral Science
Unit—and had given him the preliminary results of
their profiling of the murder scene in Milwaukee.

They'd said they figured the perp was youngish,
no more than forty, though probably closer to thirty, white, male, highly intelligent, and meticulously
neat. At least on one level he had a very orderly,
deliberate kind of mind, the kind you might assume
someone in the sciences had. On another level, of
course, his mind was in total chaos.

They also said that they had fed the third murder, that of Margaret Tatterstall, into the VICAP
computers, but had not come up with anything as
far as M.O.

The Bureau was not sure if they were dealing with a true serial murderer—it might just be someone with a particular fantasy that involved some serial-murder aspects but not all. There was sexual contact—likely postmortem—with two of the victims, but they didn't find a foreign object in the vagina, a frequent practice of serial murderers, and though the body was mutilated—the wrists slashed—the mutilation was relatively restrained. Serial murderers could work on a body like butchers worked on cows going through meat-packing plants.

The Byzantine cross had been analyzed metallurgically and both chain and cross were high-quality silver—and commonly available, as Hallstrom had learned himself.

Hallstrom had read the case file from the beginning, and had not come up with anything fresh.

His concentration was hardly complete, because he occasionally thought about Emma.

He found himself deeply concerned about her. Ridgely had reported the hallucination that Emma had had on the El station and train, and it pained him.

What bothered him too was the very real threat she faced. Ridgely was good, but Emma was unpredictable, and the killer was clever. They hadn't a clue to who he was.

And the FBI had said that one thing was for sure: The killer would seem like a very ordinary citizen. The monster inside was well hidden.

Hallstrom knew that he would kill again . . . and again until caught. For some reason he had to kill.

He rubbed his eyes, leaned back in his chair, and tried to let his mind free-float over the case details . . . and tried to hear that small inner voice that cops would listen for. A voice that was a blend of intellect and emotion and raw instinct that sometimes could yield a clue.

But he heard nothing.

Maybe, he thought, later in the day he could have a brainstorming session with Mitchell and whoever else knew the case. "Five brains are better than one," his first Homicide CO had told him, and Hallstrom was a firm believer in that.

But for now, he had nothing.

He was about to look over the photos again, when he glanced at his bulletin board. The DETECTIVES DO IT UNDERCOVER poster was obscured by several letters pinned to it. All that could be read was "DO IT."

Something far, far away in his belly spoke to him, but he could not hear it.

He got up and unpinned the letters.

One by one, he looked at them. All were addressed to Emma, though all had mistakenly gone to Valerie Wheaton's apartment.

The tiny voice in Hallstrom's stomach found another voice.

"Hospital bills," Hallstrom said out loud.

He leafed through the envelopes again.

"All the letters for Emma that came to Valerie's apartment are *hospital bills*."

Two minutes later, Hallstrom was on the street outside the precinct. It was raining pretty hard. He didn't notice.

He got in his unmarked car and a moment later was speeding down the shiny street, driving a bit too fast for the weather, but far too slow for what he wanted to see.

38

• • •

TWENTY MINUTES LATER, HALLSTROM WAS IN THE the sub-subbasement of Booth Memorial, the bowels of the building where patient records were kept. He was nervous, almost pacing back and forth as an older white-haired nurse fingered through a top filing cabinet.

The records were voluminous.

"You got records for every nosebleed in Illinois?"

Two minutes earlier he had asked for all of Emma's records.

"If you'll just be patient . . ."

She found the file and handed it to him. He placed the file on a nearby table and leafed through it rapidly—until he found what he wanted and put his finger on it, as if it would disappear if he didn't. It was Emma's apartment number—supposedly.

He looked up at the nurse.

"This says 3B."

"Yes," the nurse said.

"Emma lives in Apartment 2B."

"Someone made a mistake."

"That's right. Valerie Wheaton lived—and died—in Apartment 3B."

"I don't know what you're talking about, sir, but no one has access to these files but personnel."

"Who filled these out? This isn't Emma's writing."

"Wasn't she the blind woman, sir?"

Hallstrom nodded.

She looked at the file. "That looks like Dr. Pierce's writing."

Hallstrom looked at her, then was gone out the door.

39

. . .

THE DAY AFTER HER HALLUCINATION ON THE EL train, Emma paid an unannounced visit to the office of Dr. Ryan Pierce. As usual, her cop shadow—this time Crowe—was with her, but he stayed behind while Emma walked down a corridor with Pierce, who was on his way to surgery.

As succinctly as she could, Emma explained the ordeal on the train, the killer who'd turned out to be Ridgely, her mother—who'd disappeared, and the other woman on the train—the conductor.

"Why is this still happening? Why am I still hallucinating?"

"These things you're seeing now are not physiological, they're psychological. The apparitions you saw on that train were products of your own mind."

"You said they were from the operation. You're a psychiatrist now?"

"You were a severely abused child. You've never dealt with that."

"I miss my dog," she said.

154

• • •

LATER, EMMA WAS in the space-age–style chair in an examining room and Pierce put drops in her eyes.

"What were you doing at the El station in the middle of the night?"

"Why do you want to know?"

"Does it have anything to do with Detective Hallstrom?"

Emma surprised herself. She bristled. "Leave him out of this. You don't like him because you . . ."

"What? Wanted you for myself?"

"He didn't treat me like an invalid," she said. "Do you know what that means to me? The other night he tripped me."

"How romantic. You're ready for contacts. If you want them. Or glasses. They'll correct you to twenty-twenty."

Finished, Pierce went over to the sink, squirted some soap to his hands from a dispenser, and soaped up.

"Do you think I really saw the killer?" Emma asked.

"Seeing isn't something that happens to you, Emma, it's something you do. I gave you the equipment. It's up to you to control it. If you invent these visions, you can stop them."

Pierce started to wash his hands. "It doesn't matter what I think. What do you think?"

For a moment, he pulled his hands from the sink and faced her to better emphasize his point. Hands and forearms were lathered with the thick, pungent soap. In that moment, the smell of the soap hit her.

The smell from the hallway, from the garage.

The smell of murder.

155

Emma tried to hold it together, forgetting for the moment that Crowe was right outside.

"I'll . . . I'll call you later," she said, her voice almost croaking.

Pierce's eyes narrowed. He looked at her wonderingly as she half backed out of the room and was gone.

40
. . .

Hallstrom was in his unmarked car, tooling down Michigan Avenue, on the phone long-distance.

The connection to Milwaukee was not good, but now it cleared up. On the phone was Mike Noble, a sergeant with the Milwaukee Homicide Unit.

"Sergeant," Hallstrom said, "I'm trying to find out if Margaret Tatterstall spent any time in the hospital in the last six months."

Just at that moment, he stopped at a red light.

"A lot of time. Really?" he said after a pause.

The light turned green, but Hallstrom was oblivious to it.

"A new kidney?" he said.

He hung up, but didn't move, his mind turned inward until the blaring of horns behind him snapped him back.

The puzzle was starting to come together.

41

. . .

SHORTLY AFTER SHE HAD SEEN PIERCE, EMMA
walked—barged—into the Third Precinct, past the
uniformed desk sergeant. Crowe had to half trot to
keep up with her.

"Hey," the sergeant said, "you can't . . ."

The sergeant made a motion as if to stop Emma,
but Crowe shook his head.

"It's okay," he said.

Emma threaded her way through the squad room
and into John Hallstrom's office. He was not there.

She turned and walked away—into Mitchell's
office.

Mitchell was at his desk absorbed in some paperwork, and looked up when Emma came in.

"Can I help you?"

"Where's John?"

"What's the problem?"

"I want to talk to him."

"Why can't you tell me?"

Emma looked at him coldly. "Because I don't like you."

"I'm expecting John any minute. There's been another murder. In Indiana."

"When?"

"Just happened this morning."

"In Indiana?"

Emma sank into a chair in front of Mitchell's desk. She could imagine how this would affect John.

"Now you think you wanna tell me?" Mitchell asked.

"It's nothing. Nothing." She did not like this man. Fuck him.

She got up and headed for the door, then stopped and turned in the doorway.

"That smell," she said, "on the killer's hands. It was surgical soap. He must bring it with him. He washes his hands to get rid of the blood."

Then she was gone.

42

. . .

THE HOUSE WAS IN AN EXCLUSIVE SUBURB OF Chicago, and it very much belonged. It was made of old brick, with black trim and a pale orange tile roof, genuine copper gutters, and stained-glass windows; wrought-iron fencing surrounded the two acres of carefully landscaped greensward it was located on. It smelled of old money.

In the driveway were parked a black 1993 Jaguar, a 1992 green BMW, and—the least impressive of the cars—a new-model Ford with little or no chrome or ornamentation: the unmarked car of John Hallstrom.

The house belonged to David and Rita Getz, the parents of the the first murder victim, Nina Getz.

Hallstrom had arrived ten minutes earlier, and was talking with Mr. Getz in the mahogany-paneled, book-lined study of the house. Getz was in golf togs. He was standing next to Hallstrom in front of a large picture window.

"Mr. Getz, tell me about the scars on Nina's legs."

"But that was so long ago."

"How long?"

"When she was five, her . . . her legs were badly burned in a stable fire. She's had skin grafts for years. She was very sensitive."

"Did she have any skin grafts recently?"

"Well, just before the . . . murder, they tried a new plastic surgery, with donor skin."

"Skin from a donor . . ."

"Yes."

"Who is the doctor?"

A few minutes later, Hallstrom was tooling down the sweeping driveway that lead to the house.

IN THE WEE hours of morning, Hallstrom was in another hospital, this one Mather Central, an exclusive facility down near the lake.

Hallstrom was tired, but so was the doctor he'd had to rouse from sleep for help. They were both in the computer room of Mather, and the doctor, aside from being tired, was irksome.

"I don't like this. Nina Getz was my patient for many years."

"This man has killed four people," Hallstrom said—and realized he'd almost said three. Christ.

"These things are a matter of the strictest privacy."

Finally, the doctor stopped rolling the screen, working the keyboard.

"Here it is," he said to Hallstrom. "Leslie Davison."

Hallstrom left. Now it was all coming together. But he knew also that what was against him was what was often against cops. Something that often defeated their efforts. The clock.

43

· · ·

ALMOST ALL EVENING, EMMA'S PHONE HAD BEEN ringing, but she ignored it. She was too much into playing her violin; or more to the point, composing. She would hum a note, jot it down on staff paper, and continue.

But part of her realized that she wasn't only composing. She was starting to grieve, starting to sense that she might not ever be able to reach Hallstrom. More than once during the day, she had cried, or her eyes had misted over.

Abruptly, someone knocked on the door. John or . . .

But it wasn't. It was Dr. Pierce, with Crowe standing behind him.

"She's not gonna answer the door. Believe me, I've tried," Crowe said.

Pierce knocked again. "Emma. Please. It's Dr. Pierce . . . I've been trying to reach you all day. Why did you run off like that?"

She got up and walked to the door, mindful that Crowe was sitting outside in a chair . . . if he wasn't dead.

She did not open the door.

"Please go. I'm fine really."

She waffled. Maybe she should open it. Dr. Pierce, who was so caring, didn't make sense as a killer.

She put her hand on the knob, but still hesitated.

"Emma, listen," Pierce said, "one of the donors' families is threatening to sue. Mrs. Davison had . . . religious objections to the harvesting of her daughter's organs, even though Leslie was a voluntary donor."

Davison, Emma thought. For the first time she knew the name of the person who had given her sight.

"I don't think," Pierce continued, "that she has a case but . . . organ donors are vital. A suit like this . . ."

Pierce got a little annoyed. "Emma, are you listening? She needs to see you. See how her daughter's cornea changed your life. Because they did, Emma, whether you like it or not . . . they did."

Still, no response.

Pierce, defeated, turned away. And the door opened.

Emma was standing there.

"If I cry one more tear," she said, "I think I'll go blind."

44

. . .

JOHN HALLSTROM STOOD IN MITCHELL'S OFFICE along with Joe Beck, an agent with the FBI; David Frank, the Milwaukee cop; and Ridgely, Barry, and Mitchell himself.

They had come together rapidly when Hallstrom had said the visit to the hospital had given him the breakthrough he needed: the logic that tied the victims together.

"Margaret Tatterstall, Frank's victim, Milwaukee . . . kidney transplant, two months ago."

"So?" Frank said.

"Nina Getz had skin grafts, using skin from an organ donor. About eight weeks ago," Hallstrom responded.

"Holy fuck," Ridgely said softly.

"The postmortem wrist wounds: Coroner says blood loss speeds the decay of the organs. So they can't be passed on again."

"Valerie Wheaton never had a transplant," Frank

said, playing devil's advocate.

"But the woman who lives below her did. Corneal transplant. And her apartment number is listed incorrectly on her medical records."

Hallstrom paused. Then: "Sir, this guy meant to kill Emma Brody."

"Who the fuck is he?" Barry asked.

"I don't know yet, but I think the donor is the key. Nina Getz's donor's name was Leslie Davison. I'll bet this Davison girl is the donor for all of these victims. Getz, Tatterstall, Emma—"

"We sent Ned out to Indiana," Mitchell said. "Their victim, the latest . . . she was a heart transplant patient."

It was abundantly clear: Hallstrom was right—dead right.

"I gotta go. I got to be with her," Hallstrom said, and inside he felt relief. He was tired of fighting the pull towards Emma. He needed her, and she—not this case—was the priority.

Hallstrom left the room, Ridgely and Mitchell following him. They caught up to him before he hit the stairs.

"John, John," Mitchell said, "what the fuck are you doing? You can't walk out."

"Get this fucking task force off their asses and put 'em to work!"

Fundamentally, Mitchell and Hallstrom were friends, and Mitchell made a final appeal.

"I'll put the whole police force on her, John. The best thing you can do for her is find out who the son of a bitch is. And bring him in."

Hallstrom knew, finally, that that was the way it had to be.

45
. . .

CROWE TURNED THE BIG GREEN IMPALA HE WAS driving into Etheridge Street. The Davison address Dr. Pierce had given Emma was 123 Etheridge.

Etheridge Street could hardly be called posh.

It was in a dimly lit, basically industrial area of the city, and the street was in bad need of a sweeper. As the car moved slowly down the block, Emma and Crowe were unable to see just where anyone could live. Some of the street lights were out, and there were no stoops, porches, or other physical indications of human habitation. Just store fronts and factories.

Then it became clear. The apartments, just a few, were above the garages. The door of choice, at least on the garages, was corrugated steel, and the decor on them and the other parts of the structures had been provided by graffiti artists armed with spray cans of paint.

Crowe was quiet until they were halfway down the block and he had pulled the car to an idling stop in front of 123.

"I don't like this," he said.

"This is the right address. It must be above the garage. I'll go in."

"No. I'm gonna turn the car around down there and park across the street."

"I'll be fine. I'm getting out."

"Uh-uh. Hallstrom told me never to let you out of my sight."

Emma nodded.

"I'll wait right here," she said. "Right here where you can see me."

She got out and he pulled away. A surge of rebellion or something hit her. Fuck Hallstrom.

"I don't take Hallstrom's orders," she said to the car, which by now was a good fifty yards away.

She waited until Crowe's brake lights glowed red as he started to make a U and come back to park, then headed for the building.

Up the street, Crowe spotted her.

He made a simple comment—"Shit"—and then he honked the horn and it echoed loudly. But Emma paid no mind to him.

As Emma approached the building, she was not quite sure whether to go in a side door, or ring a bell, or . . .

She decided the best bet was to go in the entry door adjacent to the garage. She glanced up before she did. It was funny. She could see what looked like the windows of an apartment, but the lights were off.

Then, abruptly, the corrugated garage door started to clank up, and she peered into the dark maw of the interior. It was a little spooky.

She thought about waiting for Crowe, but then tried the knob on the door adjacent to the garage. It turned . . .

46
. . .

John Hallstrom was now at Booth Memorial, the hospital where Leslie Davison had been a nurse.

He had learned that on the night of February 3 Leslie had been brought into the ER after the automobile accident. She was flatline when she arrived, and though the staff worked heroically on her, they could not bring her back.

Now Hallstrom and Ridgely were going floor to floor, showing the drawing of the perp Emma had seen, hoping that someone would make him.

Hallstrom had had little luck. Now, he showed the drawing to a blond-haired nurse in the children's ward.

"I don't know," the nurse said.

"The kids would say," a dark-haired nurse said, "that he looks like a bad guy."

"There aren't any bad guys around here," the blonde said.

"Think of him," Hallstrom said, "in terms of Leslie. Someone she might have known. Someone who liked her."

"Everyone liked her. When they brought her in . . . after the accident . . . people were crying. Just sort of standing around."

Abruptly, Ridgely appeared. "I got an ID. From an orderly. The perp's name is Neal Booker."

"Did you run it?"

"It's an alias."

"Shit."

"Neal Booker?" the dark-haired nurse said. "The orderly? He's so quiet and pale . . . like he's not even there."

The nurses looked at the drawing again for what seemed a long time.

"I guess that could be Neal," the blonde said, "if he were really angry . . . and scared."

"Ridge," Hallstrom said, "get down to personnel, try to get an address on him."

Ridgely left the room immediately.

Hallstrom turned to the nurses: "Page Dr. Ryan Pierce for me."

47

· · ·

Emma CLIMBED THE STAIRS TO THE APARTMENT.

At the top, off a small landing, was a single door.

She knocked. When there was no answer she knocked again. If the woman wasn't there, who had opened the garage? Maybe she was down there.

Emma knocked one more time, then headed back to the street level.

On the street, she saw Crowe pulling the car into the garage. His lights were on, illuminating the interior. He parked next to a BMW. She stood there a moment, not sure what to do.

Then she saw Crowe stick his hand out the window and wave in an agitated kind of way. What the fuck was going on?

She went into the garage, and just as she did the corrugated door behind her started to clank down.

"What's going on?" she said to Crowe as she approached him from the driver's side of the car.

More puzzlement.

The window was now closed. Crowe had his head turned away. She tapped on the glass.

"Hey!"

The window rolled down.

Crowe turned towards her . . . and the sharp soap smell hit her.

It wasn't Crowe. It was the killer, the face on the stairs, the face in her nightmares.

She backed up, shutting her eyes tight.

"No," she said out loud. "Not again. It's Officer Crowe. It's only Crowe. This is my mind playing tricks." She stood there, forcing herself not to run. With heroic effort, she opened her eyes.

Blink.

It was Crowe. He had gotten out of the car and was standing, facing her.

Blink.

It was the killer . . . and behind him a grisly sight. It was Crowe, his throat cut, his chest splashed with blood, falling towards the front seat.

The killer looked at her, his eyes spacey, glinting: the man in the hall, in the drawing, in her dreams and nightmares. The man from yesterday and today. He held a hand out, and in it was a cross.

She turned to run—but the door was completely down. She turned.

"Can you see me, Leslie?"

She could see. But now she could not move. She could not even talk.

48

• • •

HALLSTROM STOOD IN THE CORRIDOR OUTSIDE THE operating room. Dr. Ryan Pierce came out dressed in surgical greens, a mask, and bloodstained vinyl gloves. He pulled the mask aside.

"You have thirty seconds."

"It's about Emma."

"Forty seconds."

"Emma's donor was Leslie Davison?"

"How did you get that information?"

"She has something to do with the murders."

"Yes. Leslie Davison is one of her donors. Emma's with Leslie's mother right now."

The hair on Hallstrom's neck stood up. He realized what it was.

A trap.

Miraculously, Pierce remembered the address. Hallstrom ran down the hall as fast as traffic and his legs allowed.

49

. . .

T HE MURDERER TOOK A STEP TOWARDS EMMA.

"Your eyes are different, Leslie," he said. "What have they done to your eyes?"

It was, Emma knew, her only shot. She was Leslie, or she was dead.

"They gave them to . . . her," Emma said.

He grimaced as he looked at her eyes. "They're not the right color."

"They gave her the corneas. The clear windows on top."

"The windows of the soul."

He stepped closer, grasped Emma by the shoulders. She forced herself to look. It was like looking, inches away, into the eyes of a tiger.

But she kept looking, pushing down the fear screaming inside her.

"I'm here," she said.

His mind jumped. He grasped her shoulders again.

"I've been looking for you. In all of them. I saw them . . . carry pieces of you away. Running down hallways with pieces of you in plastic boxes. But I found them. I was looking for you but they wouldn't stop screaming. I had to kill them."

Emma was going on pure instinct, a primitive logic born of the need to survive. "I'm here."

"You were covered in blood. Your face. You went through the glass. Your head broke the glass. Did it . . . did it hurt?"

Emma, terrorized as she was, could recall the pain—her own pain. Her eyes teared, as much from fear as memory.

"Yes," she said.

"Don't cry, Leslie. You see me?"

"Yes."

"You never looked at me before. But I knew you knew. Your buttons undone. For me. Little pearl buttons. I could see your breasts. Silver laying there beside them."

He held up a cross. "Put it on."

Emma took the cross. Her hands were trembling, and she had trouble with the clasp. Each moment was forever. His eyes, flat, thin windows just in front of homicidal rage, bored into her.

Abruptly, the radio coughed.

"One-charlie-niner, one-charlie-niner . . . what is your location. Do you read?"

The killer glanced back at the radio—and Emma made a decision and swung her foot up with all the force she could muster, driving it into his crotch . . . and then jumped past him inside the car—onto the bloody corpse of Crowe . . .

She grabbed the radio.

"I'm in a . . . a garage on the South . . ."

But like a cat and despite the immenseness of his pain, he reached and snapped off the antenna, and the radio went dead.

She realized she hadn't succeeded.

But knew she would be better than he was in one environment—and she found the headlight knob and slammed it in, and the garage went black.

Now, she heard him coming for her in the darkness, but it was not a smooth journey, and he bumped into the car and yowled as Emma searched for what to do. What to do?

It was seconds, it was forever, Emma moving slightly from her position in the front seat, and then the lights went on and she spotted him in the rearview mirror, and then she knew what to do and searched, her hands slimy with warm blood, for Crowe's gun—and found it.

She looked into the rearview mirror, hoping to spot the killer. But it was not him. It was her. Nine years old.

God. Don't fail me now.

She wrenched herself out of the car, saw him, pointed the gun . . .

Blink. It was John Hallstrom. Had he come in, was it a hallucination . . .

"John!"

"John" spoke, the words slithering out of his mouth, the sounds and rhythm of a killer. "You're not Leslie. You're one of them. You killed her to give you life."

Emma could not bear to look at him. She knew she must. Must.

There was no doubt. It was the killer.

"Look at him," she screamed.

She fired, and the sound boomed in the garage and she'd missed, and fired again and backed away, and fired again and missed, and now he was coming close to her and almost had her, and words came out of him, low and filled with venom.

"That fucking sow who had her heart. Her little beating heart working so hard in that fat flesh . . ."

What was it? Why was she missing? God, she didn't know who she was really shooting at—or not shooting at. Maybe at a hallucination . . .

Emma glanced up. The light! She fired. The garage went black.

IN THEIR UNMARKED, siren hammering, Hallstrom and Ridgely screamed down a southside street.

"She'll be all right," Ridgely said lamely.

"You shoulda let me go. You should have let me go to her."

But Hallstrom knew it was not Ridgely's fault, or Mitchell's. It was his. He'd doubted her, he'd abused her, he'd walked away when she needed him most.

But the dam had burst inside him for good, and if she died, if this fuck killed her, a big part of himself would go with her.

He had to save her—and himself.

She needed him now . . . now more than ever.

EMMA HAD HEARD the siren, and was filled with hope . . . if only she could evade the killer till help arrived.

Then the unmarked was outside the garage and she was home free and she screamed.

"I'm here! I'm here!"

"I hear you." It was the murderer, the voice of a madman.

She felt his hand brush against her, and then she dropped to the floor and rolled under the BMW.

But Hallstrom and Ridgely banged up the stairs and rapped against the apartment door, and no one answered and they took the door down . . .

And the apartment was empty . . .

God, where was she?

IN THE GARAGE, the killer hunted her, unmindful, not caring about cops, his mind focused on one thing: to crush the life from Emma, to open her veins, so no one could use Leslie anymore . . .

But he couldn't find her . . . and he pounded the front of the BMW in rage and screamed—

"WHERE ARE YOU!!!"

—and triggered the car alarm. Suddenly the lights were flashing, the horn honking, and he spotted her under the car and ran around to grab her. Emma waited, her hands slick, and rolled out just before he grabbed her, and then was up and pointed the gun at him.

Blink.

"No," Emma said.

It was not the killer coming at her, but the contorted, enraged face of her mother!

Blink.

No. It was the killer.

No. Her mother.

He was almost upon her—the lights going on and off, on and off, like some super-fast slide show, the horn yammering, and she started to cry and something deep, deep inside her surged up . . .

"Goddammit, no," she screamed. "No."

It was him. No doubt. The danger was real . . .

She squeezed the trigger three times—and blood spurted from his chest and he fell, as if in slow motion, the flashing lights freeze-framing as he went . . .

Then to her left the garage door was being lifted manually . . . by Hallstrom and Ridgely.

And then it was open and Emma saw him and dropped the gun and walked over to him, and there were tears in his eyes and they ran down his cheeks, and he took her in his arms like he would hold her forever, and he would.

50

· · ·

BACKUP AND PARAMEDICS HAD ARRIVED EN MASSE
a few minutes after the near-fatal encounter in
the garage. In the ensuing hubbub Emma got separated from Hallstrom, but knew she would see him
again.

LATER AT THE precinct, in Mitchell's office, Emma
was questioned by a team from the precinct, then
the FBI. It was all very brief, and then it was over.

"You can go, Miss Brody," Mitchell said. "You sure
you don't want to check into the hospital?"

"I think I've had enough of the hospital."

"Should we call your friend?"

"It's a little early for her."

"I'll drop you," Ridgely said.

Ridgely led Emma out of the station, and they
were about to get into his car when Emma stopped.

Hallstrom was across the street—with a four-
footed surprise.

Ralph still was bandaged up, and the effects of nonstop investigative work were etched in Hallstrom's face.

Emma laughed. A motley pair, she thought.

"I think," Emma said to Ridgely, "I've got a way home."

"YOU CAUGHT THE killer," Hallstrom said as they walked along.

Emma smiled wearily.

"Figured the least I could do," Hallstrom said, "was write you some lyrics."

"What?"

He pulled a tattered envelope out of his jacket pocket. Slowly, with deep feeling, he read.

"Light in Emma's eyes/Rescued roses from my hands/Made them bloom again."

She swallowed hard.

"That's all I got, so far," he said.

That's far enough, Emma thought, far enough . . . and squeezed his hand.

Then Hallstrom stopped, picked up a stick, and threw it. Ralph loped after it. He was going to be all right.

51

· · ·

HALLSTROM PUT IT ALL TOGETHER LATER, AND
when he did it gave him a chill . . . or two.

Neal Booker—real name James Butler, it turned
out—had spent some serious time in a mental
facility in Iowa before arriving at Booth Memorial
Hospital, and when they tossed his apartment they
found considerable material showing his adoration
of and obsession with Leslie Davison, from one of
her uniform caps he had stolen to telephoto pictures
he had taken of her . . . almost five hundred in all.

It was all arranged in a closet that he had made
into a kind of grotto, or altar.

But they also found much other material indicating, as Mitchell put it, that he "was two quarts low."
There was pornography, accounts of murder—and
more crosses. And as it happened, Leslie Davison
had donated seven organs of her body. If they had
not stopped Butler/Booker, he could have killed even
more.

But what really chilled Hallstrom was the setup.

This maniac had done it so perfectly, luring Emma into a trap, but then, when he could have killed her, he hadn't.

Maybe just the week earlier Hallstrom could not have begun to understand. Now he did. Butler's need to have Leslie Davison alive had overpowered all sense of reality he had . . . which was not much to begin with.

Yeah, Hallstrom thought, when you need badly enough, you can make it all come true in your mind.

And Emma. What she had endured. Neither he nor she could explain exactly what had happened to her, except to say that sight had made the terrors in her past emerge to merge with terrors in the present. She had been safe in the blackness, but going forward had brought her into the light . . . terrifying light.

She had made him laugh when she said, "Most people are afraid of the dark. Not Emma. She's afraid of the light!"

Well, at some point she would get some counseling, she said, so she could be sure to keep her terrors straight.

All this Hallstrom thought as he sat at a table in the Algonblick Pub and watched Emma and the Drovers jam.

She was really working the violin, the sound sweet, and then she looked over at him with those beautiful eyes that made his insides go a little hollow, and he knew she saw him—for what he really was. She had him dead to rights.

Which, quite simply, was a man in love.